TRYING TO REASON WITH
HURRICANE
SEASON

TRYING TO REASON WITH
HURRICANE SEASON

CHIP BELL

WORD ASSOCIATION PUBLISHERS
www.wordassociation.com
1.800.827.7903

Printed in the United States of America.

ISBN: 978-1-59571-732-0

Library of Congress Control Number: 2011940413

Designed and published by

Word Association Publishers
205 Fifth Avenue
Tarentum, Pennsylvania 15084

www.wordassociation.com
1.800.827.7903

"Hurricane Season in the Atlantic begins June 1
and ends November 30."
–National Hurricane Center

"Squalls out on the Gulf Stream, big storm's coming soon…"
–"Trying to Reason with Hurricane Season"
–Jimmy Buffett

To Mike, for that first CD and concert, and all the rest.

ACKNOWLEDGEMENT

Once again, to Eve, for all her listening, typing, and re-typing; once again to Cynthia Nelson for editing my manuscript into a much better book; to Gloria Thompson for her proofreading skills; and to Tom Costello and the staff at Word Association for helping me take my shot.

TRYING TO REASON WITH

HURRICANE
SEASON

JUNE

CHAPTER 1

The two old men sat in silence in the ornate room, their faces illuminated only by the table lamp between them. Fatigue weighed on their shoulders like a cloak soaked by the rain.

The daylong battle was finally over. The arguments, the screaming, the threats, and the recriminations—all had given way to what they had finally been able to agree on through the sheer force of their personalities.

Slowly, the older of the two rose and made his way to the balcony and looked out over the city. The lights glistened as nightlife began stirring in the Vedado and the ships lying at anchor in the Malecón slowly rocked to and fro in their berths as a warm breeze moved through the June night.

Looking at the illuminated sculpture of Che Guevara on the Ministry of the Interior, he wondered what his good friend, who had fought by his side for so long and who died fighting for the revolution he believed in, would have thought about what they were about to do. His thoughts went back to those times, and the times since when he stood on this balcony and shouted the words of the Revolution to the thousands beneath him in the square. Urging them to be true to the beliefs of the Revolution and to understand their enemy was the United States, the great capitalist giant to the north. He had been the face of that Revolution, the leader known around the world for his fiery oratory and his refusal to surrender his beliefs.

How had it come to this? How could they do what they were about to do?

Shaking his head in sadness, Fidel Castro turned to his brother Raul. "You know this means the end of everything we have ever believed in, everything we have fought for. We are turning our backs on the Revolution, our heroes, and everything they stand for. We are going back to 1959 when that bastard Batista played the puppet and danced on the American strings."

Raul Castro, who two days ago had celebrated his 81st birthday, had been President of Cuba since 2008 when his older brother Fidel, who would be 86 years old in August, stepped down for reasons of health. He heard his brother's words and he understood his passions. Fidel had always been the passionate one, the one with the gift for soaring rhetoric, fist pounding speeches, and the ability to make the people follow him. Raul was the thoughtful one, the one who implemented plans to try and help the country and make things work.

He sighed. They both had failed. He knew in his heart that Fidel's beliefs in communism had been proven wrong and he knew that no matter what plans he had implemented, they had failed their people, they had failed Cuba. Raul turned in his chair and replied to his brother, "Fidel we have to do this. We have tried everything. It is time to admit our mistakes. It is time to save our people. Cuba is bankrupt. Our people are poor, starving, uneducated. Sickness and disease are growing among the population, and there is no money to provide them with the basic necessities of life. What we do now is not going back to Batista. We are going to make this country a democracy. We are going to let the people speak for what they want. Fidel, think what has happened over the years. Have we not become that which we replaced? Have we not ruled this country with an iron fist, allowing no one to speak against us? Have we made this country the country of its people or our country?"

Fidel Castro's eyes filled with rage. He summoned the strength he had left, slammed his hand on the railing of the balcony and turned on his brother. "Do not lecture me, Raul! We had no choice. It wasn't we who betrayed the Revolution, it was the Russians. They perverted communism for their own ends and became worse than the capitalists! They tied us to their side like a raft to a great ocean liner and sailed as they chose, taking us with them. And then when they foundered and begin to sink under the might of the United States they took Cuba to the bottom with them! You know our original plan was to consolidate power only to give it back to the people after the system had been put in place and it was working."

"That's just the point, Fidel. It never worked. The system never worked. You never understood that the simplest peasant is happiest not when the government is plotting the course of his life, but when he has the liberty to choose for himself, to own his own small piece of ground, but be equal under the law to those who own the wealthiest estates."

"Rubbish!" yelled Fidel." What you say means the poor will always be poor and the rich will always be rich. There can be no freedom for anyone who has to grovel before those with money, because money gives power; undeserved power to rule over others. The wealthy in Miramar and Siboney will always rule the peasants in the field."

"Fidel, we ruled over others. We held the power. It never got to the people."

"Only because our enemies strangled us and never let the system flourish."

Raul shook his head. Fidel was a true believer. It had taken him months to convince Fidel of the course they had to take, what they had to do, because without his agreement there could be no agreement with anyone else in Cuba. He pled his case again and again. He used numbers, statistics, took Fidel on tours of the countryside, made him see what was going on in the country, and finally begged him... begged him to do what they had to do to save Cuba, and finally Fidel had agreed.

Fidel knew that Raul's silence meant the argument was over, and once again, he had lost. He turned and looked out over the city again. He knew that the path Raul had chosen was right, that it was their only hope, the only course of action open to them. But more than anything, he knew that he had failed... failed himself, failed his brother, his people, and Cuba. It left a bitter taste in his mouth, made more bitter by the fact now he had to turn to his most despised enemy, the capitalist giant of the north, to save Cuba. Feeling every bit of his 86 years, he slowly walked back to his chair and slumped down. He reached across and patted the arm of his brother Raul, whom he still so dearly loved." Make the call to President Fletcher, Raul. Do what we have to do."

CHAPTER 2

The June night was warm in Camp David, Maryland, more humid than was normal this time of year outside of Washington, D. C. Perspiration was wetting the backs of the shirts of the Secret Service Agents making their rounds. Fireflies would occasionally catch the eye of the ever-observant agents as they peered into the dark woods surrounding the cabin where President Jordan Fletcher and his trusted Chief of Staff sat and waited.

Jordan Fletcher, President of the United States, had been elected to a second term in a landslide the previous year. Benjamin Matthews, his rival for the presidency, had been almost assured of winning until a trial had exposed what his chief contender had been up to and how close their country had come to being governed by a madman. Fletcher spoke to Jason Bates, his Chief of Staff." Well, Jason, will he make the call?"

"He will, Mr. President."

"What makes you so sure? Fidel Castro has a long and abiding hatred for this country. To him, we are the personification of evil capitalism; the ones that put a noose around him early and kept squeezing 'til the last breath."

"Mr. President, I firmly believe that politics is based upon realistic choices, and Fidel and Raul Castro have no other choice."

"I don't know Jason. Maybe we boxed them in too tightly. Maybe we should have given them an option."

"Mr. President, we have spent three months working out every detail of the treaty to be entered into between Cuba and the United States. Every time we made a proposal and it was agreed upon, there would be a new demand to change something previously agreed upon. The final document is in the best interests of both countries, but most importantly, in the best interest of the United States. The only way to get this agreement finalized was to give Fidel and Raul Castro notice that there will be no more changes, and today, June 5, would be the last day that we would accept the treaty as written, and after that, there would be no treaty."

"I know, Jason. But I know what I'm like when someone tries to box me in. My first instinct is to fight my way out and not accept terms that have been shoved down my throat."

"Mr. President, these terms are far from being shoved down their throats. As I said, they were negotiated over a three-month period and serve Cuba very well. The economic aid we intend to put into that country will immediately give the Cubans a better life. The fact that the treaty calls for a democratic government to be established in Cuba and for the Castro brothers to step down and not participate in that government, for free elections to be allowed and monitored by the United Nations, will provide the citizens of Cuba with a life better than they've ever had."

"I know Jason. You sound like you're giving the speech I have to give to the American people. But, it's not a bad deal for us, either. We get permanent military bases in Cuba, a mutual non-aggression pact, a right to allow up to 30% of the Cuban gross national product to be based upon American investments in the island, and the right of the Cuban people in ten years to take a vote as to whether or not they want to become a territory of the United States."

Bates replied, "With all respect sir, of course it's not a bad deal for the United States. That's your job—to get the best deal you possibly can for the United States. You also get to end this stand-off that's been going on for over half a century. A standoff, no less, that has allowed a hostile government to exist 90 miles from our shores in violation of the Monroe Doctrine. The plans you hope to present to Congress for more oil exploration in the farther reaches of the Gulf will be vastly improved once the drilling operations can operate out of Cuba rather than the United States. And, the treaty will also give us much more sway with the Organization of American States and the rest of the nations in the Caribbean and South America."

"Jason, I know you're right, and I appreciate your passion, and I appreciate all the work you did on this. We said this second term we were going to try and do big things since we had some public support out there and Congress doesn't seem to be in the mood to give us too much trouble. It seems like yesterday that Raul Castro sent a secret envoy to me with the request that we lift the embargo and see if we could somehow enter into an agreement where U. S. aid could begin flowing into his country again."

"And you were correct, Mr. President, to realize that this was the chance for a major restructuring of the political dynamic in the entire hemisphere, rather than simply a moral obligation to provide financial aid to another country on the verge of economic collapse."

Fletcher sat back on the couch with a sigh and took a sip from the glass of scotch he had been nursing throughout the evening. "I just hope it works … I just hope it works."

The phone that had been installed solely for this purpose rang fifteen minutes later. Both Bates and Fletcher startled at the initial ring and looked at each other, their faces a mixture of anticipation and fear. Bates slowly reached for the phone and picked up the receiver.

"Jason Bates, Chief of Staff to President Fletcher... yes, yes, certainly. Good evening to you, Mr. President. Please hold for the President of the United States." Bates looked at Fletcher as he handed him the receiver. "Mr. President, President Castro of Cuba is on the line."

Their conversation did not take long. Raul Castro was quick and to the point. The treaty would be accepted on the terms presented during the last negotiating session. It was agreed that it would be implemented the last week of October and that Raul and Fidel Castro would come to Miami, where the treaty signing would be held.

"Thank you, Mr. President," Fletcher said, and hung up the phone. He rose and walked past Bates, clapping him on the shoulder as he did so, and went to put another drop of scotch into his glass. "I believe a celebratory drink is in order, Jason. We've actually done it. Cuba has agreed to the terms of the treaty."

"As I *hoped* they would, Mr. President. As I hoped they would." Jason Bates was a smart political infighter and knew that nothing was a sure thing in politics, despite his earlier bravado.

Bates waited until Fletcher had walked over to his desk and sat down.

"The one thing I am surprised at, sir, is how readily they agreed to the place and the date of the treaty signing ceremony, given its significance relative to the missile crisis in 1962."

"Jason, that's something that Raul Castro actually brought up. As you know, we wanted it because we figured we'd be out of hurricane season and it would be a show of thanks to the Cuban population of Florida who have fought so hard for Castro's removal, and who have given us so much support in past elections. President Castro made it clear to me that he believes Cuba has been unjustly held responsible for bringing the world to the brink of nuclear war back in 1962. I believe he sees this as a chance to amend the historical record; that Cuba was nothing more than a pawn in the game being played out between the Soviets and us. This treaty will end the Castros' reign in Cuba, and I think President Castro is trying to salvage his place in history."

Bates replied, "Well, sir, I believe that this October's historical moment involving Cuba and the United States will be full of hope rather than the fear of worldwide death and destruction."

Fletcher sat back in his chair, took a sip from his scotch, and thought about the possibilities.

"You use the word hope, Jason. I truly hope you're right."

JULY

CHAPTER 3

News of the treaty between Cuba and the United States was released on July 4th—with a full appreciation of the symbolic significance. All that week the world was abuzz with reaction. Leaders in Congress uniformly praised President Fletcher for ending the half-century long stalemate, even if the opposition leaders were a little grudging. There was the usual international mix of praise and condemnation, and the right-wing talk shows extolled the treaty as a victory of capitalism over communism—the actions of the administration a mere footnote to the success.

Ratification of the treaty seemed assured, so Fletcher's administration began planning for the signing ceremony while basking in the generally favorable reviews of what had been accomplished.

In the Federal Supermax Prison in Florence, Colorado, one observer of national politics was decidedly unhappy by the turn of events. Benjamin Matthews sat working a crossword puzzle while he mulled over the news. President Jordan Fletcher, he thought, the national hero.

After Fletcher and Matthew's favorite federal prosecutor, Jake Sullivan, had given him a royal screwin', he now was looking at multiple life prison terms in this god-awful place.

Meanwhile, Fletcher got to bask in the glow of public adoration. The press and the liberals lauded his successes. He had negotiated an effective treaty with Mexico and Columbia over the drug war, his economic policy was working, and the investments coming out of this deal with Cuba would certainly push it forward. He had won the re-election in a landslide, and now, he would probably go down as a great President.

What a load of crap! It all should have been his. He should have been sitting in the Oval Office, and if he had, he sure as hell wouldn't have helped the Castro brothers. Fletcher and Sullivan. They had snatched the Presidency from his grasp. His system for running the country, a workable corporate model, would have safeguarded U.S. dominance for years, and not left the country vulnerable to untrustworthy alliances. His hands clenched, and the pencil snapped. He paced, breathing deeply to calm himself. Patience.

Finally calm, he sat down at the small table in his cell, placed the breakfast tray in front of him and prepared to eat. Powdered eggs, cold limp bacon, dry toast... Matthews smiled as he fingered the packets of pepper for his eggs. Nope, there is no justice... at least not yet.

CHAPTER 4

A penlight illuminated a keyboard in the dark prison library. A few keystrokes and a secret digital password, encrypted into the system several years ago, gave the user access to the Federal database, allowing both data retrieval and data entry. Connecting to the federal storage facility in West Virginia provided access to a wealth of sensitive data: personnel files of all federal employees, including the Secret Service, members of the National Security Agency, the FBI, the United States Marshals Service, and the Justice Department.

The guard on duty at "The Farm" sat at a desk with multiple screens. He never noticed the brief flicker at the bottom of one of the screens. In seconds, records were accessed, crosschecked, and a match was found. The penlight in the prison library went off.

CHAPTER 5

Jake Sullivan had not slept much since the phone call he had received the day before. Jake had been working at his desk on a rather mundane tax fraud case when Eva had burst into the room.

"Jake, you have a call."

"And . . . ?"

"Jake, it's important."

"It better be. Who's so important that I have to interrupt my study of violations of the Internal Revenue Code?" Jake asked with a smile.

Eva never missed a beat. "How about the President of the United States?"

Jake knew from Eva's expression that she wasn't kidding, and he paused for a moment. "Yeah, I think you're right. I better take that one. Send him through."

Working with Jake Sullivan to put Benjamin Matthews behind bars had proved to the President that Jake was a man who could be trusted, and his attention to detail and his refusal to give up when challenged made him a force to be reckoned with. It hadn't hurt that since the President had reinstated Jake as Chief Prosecutor in the Miami Office of the Justice Department he had won a string of cases without a loss—all on top of his successful prosecution of

Benjamin Matthews, their common nemesis. Jake's concern that security details and treaty signing ceremonies were a little out of his purview didn't make a dent in the President's determination that Jake would run the show in Miami, and in the end, he acquiesced to the President's demands.

So, Jake Sullivan, Federal Prosecutor, was now the coordinator of all the federal agencies for the planning and security of the momentous event that was to be held just over three months from now. He quickly enlisted Mike Lang, his investigator, as second in command, and assigned all his case responsibilities to other prosecutors in the department. Then, he began assembling the team that would determine how and when the event would take place.

Jake was not surprised when he was met with skepticism by the leaders of the other security agencies who had spent their lives dealing with situations such as this and who now had to take orders from a federal prosecutor. He was just glad it wasn't total resentment. Fortunately, Jake's reputation in the Matthews' affair stood him in good stead and his relationship with the President and the President's Chief of Staff, Jason Bates, meant that interference was not going to be an issue.

However, as Jake lay awake, he had to admit to a little self-doubt. Did he really have any idea what he was doing and how he was going to pull this off? He looked over at Linda sleeping next to him. They had gone out to dinner to discuss the girls and she had decided to stay over. As Jake followed the outline of her body under the sheet, she slept quietly, unaware of his study. He wondered if things would ever get back to the way they had been. They obviously cared about each other very much, but they were still apart. Linda wasn't ready for that final reconciliation. He knew in his heart that the affair with Benjamin Matthews had had an indelible impact. Jake had almost been killed and had killed. He knew that Linda sensed he had become a different person from the man she had originally married, a person she still loved, but a person who had changed nonetheless.

Quietly, Jake slipped out of bed, padded through his apartment to the kitchen, and turned on the coffee maker. He looked at the picture on the refrigerator of his two girls, Jen and Jessie, clowning around as usual. Jen was now residing in Homestead teaching school and her husband was working for the state. Jessie was going to the University of Miami and living on campus. How old his girls had gotten, he thought, and then laughed, "How old I've gotten." It was good to have them nearby and to be able to see them so often. And, even though they weren't what the statisticians would call a normal family unit, the love was there and that's what mattered most.

Making sure the volume was down, Jake turned on the little TV in the kitchen. The news was full of reports about tropical storm Caroline, the third of the season, having the potential to evolve into a hurricane. The usual computer tracking offered multiple courses for the storm, one of which had it heading directly to the Miami-Florida Keys area. Great, thought Jake, here I am planning one of the biggest parties of the century and I have to do it in the middle of hurricane season. Just then, Linda entered the kitchen, came up behind him and wrapped her arms around his waist.

Sinking into her hug, Jake said, "I'm sorry, hon, I didn't mean to wake you."

"Another sleepless night?"

"No, I got some sleep. I just have a lot on my mind with this treaty signing ceremony."

Linda went over and poured herself a cup of coffee and smiled at him mischievously. "That's what happens when you become best friends with the President of the United States."

Jake smiled back. "I don't think I've reached best friends status yet. Close though." And they both laughed.

Jake noticed the seriousness that came into Linda's eyes. "Jake, with the Castros coming here, and the President being here, you don't think anything will happen, do you?"

There it was. Linda's sense of unease was palpable. Jake recognized the undercurrent in their current relationship: Danger accompanied Jake's work, and that element hadn't been there before.

"Linda, seriously, there is going to be so much security at this thing that no one would dare try anything. Besides, hon, I told you the President invited you and the girls to attend the ceremony. You don't think I'm going to let some crazy with a gun get anywhere near my family, do you? Based upon all reports I've gotten from the security services, threats have been minimal. Nothing out of the ordinary. Hell, practically everybody in the country, especially in the Cuban community, is ecstatic about what the President's done. Ok, the crazies will be running around, but they won't get within a mile of the President, the Castros, or anyone else. They're just going to have to be satisfied with calling the talk shows and ranting and raving like they always do." Jake could tell by the look on Linda's face that she still had her doubts. He crossed over to her, gave her a hug and tried to lighten the mood. "And don't forget, the President's best friend is in charge of everything, so what could go wrong?" And with that, she punched him in the ribs.

"I have to prep lesson plans for my summer school session, and you have to go make sure that nothing happens between the United States and Cuba between now and October." She kissed him quickly and headed for the shower, leaving Jake standing there thinking how much he loved his wife, wishing he could erase the distance between them.

The TV caught Jake's attention. The commentators were talking about the upcoming ceremony, lamenting the fact that only a limited number of press passes were going to be issued for the worldwide media that was so intent on covering the event. Washing out his cup, he thought about the long days and nights that lay ahead of him, in service to his "best friend", President Jordan Fletcher.

CHAPTER 6

It was late at night and the storeroom was stifling as Eduardo Rivera scoured the shelves for the package. He had started working in the prison kitchen that morning. Two nights before a note had been dropped through his jail cell bars telling him what was going to occur and to be ready. The next day a gringo who had worked in the kitchen had been shived in the courtyard and he was selected to take his place. Last night, instructions, a key, a small knife, and a roll of tape had been under his pillow when he went to bed. He had waited until the middle of the night, and found his cell door unlocked, as promised. Using a back stairway to the kitchen, he encountered no guards, no one. He had slowly entered the kitchen, worried that there might be guards who had come in looking for something to drink or eat, but there was no one there. The section reserved for them had an "out of order" sign placed on the coffee maker with a note that it would be up and running in the morning. The storeroom was always locked, not even the guards were trusted, but the key he had been given easily opened the door, just as promised. Here he was, sweating his balls off, sneaking around at night, in prison. Not so long ago, he had been living in a palace in Mexico, a lieutenant for one of the drug cartels. Then, he was arrested and extradited under the new treaty between the United

States and Mexico. But he knew his time was coming. He had been promised. President Fletcher and President Carbone be damned.

The boxes of pepper packages all looked the same, but he knew to look in the back row. There it was. A box with a small blue "x" on the side. Opening the box with the knife that had been under his pillow, he found what he was looking for...three pepper packets in a sealed plastic bag stuffed in the middle of the box. He removed the plastic bag, taped the box back up, and placed it on top of the stack. Putting the plastic bag in his pocket, he exited the storeroom, locked the door, and made his way back to his cell the same way as he had come.

CHAPTER 7

Jonathan Clark appraised himself in the mirror—a little bit of skin around his chin, not too much of a roll around his middle— not bad for approaching fifty. Precisely, he attached his gun and his shield to his belt over his left hip and put on his neatly pressed suit coat. It was the way Jonathan Clark lived his life. Single, his apartment reflected who he was. Antique nautical figurines and artifacts, bespeaking his love of the ocean, were perfectly arranged. Nothing was out of place. It was tasteful but not ostentatious. Clark reached up and straightened his tie with his left hand, making sure it sat perfectly in his collar. He took pride in his appearance. He took pride in his work. His work was his life. Facing another hot and humid day in Washington, D. C., he was glad he would be inside the White House all day, sitting in the air conditioning. Fortunately, "Hawk", the Secret Service code word for President Fletcher, had no outside speaking engagements planned. As long as nothing unexpected happened, it would be an office day for the President's detail. Clark would spend his day combing through incoming data from all available sources to determine if there was a viable threat against the life of the President of the United States. This was standard operating procedure, a daily responsibility. But, with the treaty signing in Miami less than three months away, he was being extra vigilant. He was good at what he did, and had a reputation for being able to categorize threats according to those which were simply the outcries of crazies, those who were venting anger, those who had actual animosity toward the President, or those who would actually carry out a chance to harm or kill him. Fortunately, there were relatively few of the last category and he had been instrumental in diffusing at least three of those, which had heightened his reputation in the agency. That was his job. He was a threat assessment analyst. In a couple months, he would go to the site and start working with all the other security forces in setting up the advance logistics for the arrival of President Fletcher and the arrival of Fidel and Raul Castro. He wasn't quite sure yet how he felt about taking orders from a federal prosecutor. He had read about Jake Sullivan and about his handling of the affair with Benjamin Matthews. He had to admit the guy had done a hell of a job, but he also knew about his somewhat sketchy past. All investigations seemed to indicate that Jake no longer drank and he had been winning case after case out of the Federal Prosecutor's Office in Miami, but taking care of the President was a whole different thing and he hoped Jake would be a help and not a hindrance to what he had to do.

Finishing his coffee, he washed his cup in the sink, dried it, and put it back in its proper place in the cupboard. The action was reflective of Clark and how he approached his job protecting the President. Everything was precise; no clutter, efficiency, and following a strict routine.

Making sure his door was locked, he went downstairs to the underground garage, retrieved his government car, and headed out. As was his routine, he would stop at Clyde's for his morning paper and his second cup of coffee, proceed to the White House and the Secret Service briefing room, review all the assignments for the day, and take up his station in guarding the most powerful man in the world.

CHAPTER 8

Clyde Johnson did not look his sixty-three years. A thin wiry black man, he had owned his corner coffee shop/newsstand for over forty years. He considered his regulars as family, and looked forward to greeting them every day with his big gapped-tooth smile, a hearty hello, and a warm cup of coffee.

Cutting open a bundle of newspapers and setting them out, he was already sweating. It was going to be a hot one today in D.C. He had just finished opening the stack with the headline about Hurricane Caroline and its potential path to Miami when the car pulled up that he knew belonged to Mr. Clark. He already had a folded copy of the *Washington Post* and readied a cup of coffee to go with one sugar and two creams.

"Clyde, how are you today?"

"Great, Mr. Clark. Startin' to sweat, though. It'll be one of those muggy days in D. C."

"Clyde, did you ever think about how much hot coffee you sell on these hot, muggy days and how the whole population of this city must be crazy?"

Clyde laughed. "People in this town been drinkin' coffee like it was water for as long as I can remember. I don't think that's ever gonna change."

"You know, Clyde, you're probably right. I know I'm not gonna change, not as long as you keep making the best coffee in D.C."

As he took the bills from Jonathan Clark, knowing that he wanted no change, Clyde answered, "I hope you don't, Mr. Clark. I'd miss you comin' by every day."

"You don't have to worry about that, Clyde. I'll see you tomorrow."

Clyde Johnson watched Jonathan Clark get into his vehicle and just as he was about to pull away, his vehicle was rear-ended by a panel truck. He saw Clark get out of his car, obviously annoyed, and move toward the driver of the truck. Just then, two men approached his stall.

Clyde, wanting every customer to become a regular, turned on the charm.

"Good morning, gentlemen. Hot coffee on a hot day, with the hot news of the day."

The taller of the two men chuckled and said, "Sounds good. Make mine black."

"Me, too," said the second man, who had picked up a copy of the *Washington Post* and opened it.

Momentarily, Clyde forgot about Mr. Clark's minor accident, besides which, the guy with the paper was blocking his view. Clyde filled two cups with steaming hot black coffee, snapped on the plastic lids, and set them down in front of his customers.

"That'll be $2. 50 for the coffee and $1. 00 for the paper."

"Oh, that's okay, I saw what I needed. I really don't want the paper," said the second man.

"Sir…my policy is if you stand here and read the paper, you bought the paper."

The man looked at him and Clyde was surprised by the hardness in his face, which was quickly replaced with a smile.

"I guess that's only fair. Sam, why don't you pay the man?"

The first gentleman, whose name was now Sam, pulled a ten out of his pocket, set it in front of Clyde, and said, "Keep the change."

Then the two men walked away.

Clyde looked over toward the accident just in time to see Mr. Clark's vehicle and the panel truck pulling away. "Well, that's good," he said, as he went back to stacking his papers and getting ready for another hot day in Washington, D. C.

CHAPTER 9

Mike Lang, who had left the FBI to become Jake Sullivan's investigator for the Miami Office of the Justice Department, sat in Jake's office while Jake stood and looked out the window behind his desk.

"Mike, it's early July and we have three and a half months to get ready. We have to coordinate every goddamn agency in the federal government, all of whom are at each other's throats half the time, to protect not only the President of the United States, but the President of Cuba and his even more famous brother—both of whom, I might add, are hated by half the population of this city. Then, there are all the other dignitaries who are going to attend, to say nothing of my wife and two girls." He turned around and looked at Mike. "So tell me, how are we going to pull this one off?"

"Jake, you're gonna do what you always do. You're gonna walk over to the conference room where the heads of all these agencies are assembled and with the utmost charm and humility admit that you have no idea what the hell you're doin' and beg 'em for help."

Jake couldn't help but laugh. "So, you want me to do it by telling the truth, huh?"

"You never can tell. It just might work."

All in all, the meeting didn't go too badly. Jake introduced himself and Mike and quickly acknowledged the unspoken doubts in the room. He admitted that security details for the President of the United States and leaders of other nations was not in his normal job description as a federal prosecutor, but that he had been given this task by the President of the United States and he intended to see it through. He wasn't going to do it alone and he would rely upon all of them for their input and their advice. He explained that he had selected North Shore Park along Collins Avenue as the site for the ceremony, given the fact that it was flanked by the ocean on one side and Collins Avenue on the other. It was an area that could be easily cordoned off and sealed. There was only one row of buildings along the other side of Collins Avenue that would have to be protected to take away any sniper angles. Additionally, the Coast Guard could provide coverage on the water side, leaving only the northern and southern ends of the park and the Collins Avenue side to be guarded by the other security agencies. It was basically a green, flat area with some trees that would offer maximum visibility for security personnel, and no area from which a perpetrator could launch an attack. After some discussion, those in attendance agreed that the assessment and site selection had been done with thoughtful planning and excellent threat assessment. The reaction was what Jake had hoped for. He had established credibility, and earned a level of confidence, especially after he had made it clear that he considered them the experts and he would listen to their suggestions. The agency heads were quick to divide up responsibilities and parcel out areas for surveillance. Jake assigned Mike as the coordinator between the various agencies. He requested that Mike receive daily briefing papers from the heads of the various agencies, which he would review and then give to Jake. Sullivan also made it clear that he would meet with the agency heads at any time should they feel it necessary to review any item regarding the planning of the event. He could tell that his accessibility also won points with the agency heads.

Jake indicated that after receiving the initial briefing papers from the various agencies, he would synthesize the recommendations and try to establish an hour-by-hour schedule for the event and create a list of what needed to be done on a week-by-week basis prior to the event. Then he would schedule the next meeting. This appeared to be satisfactory to all in attendance and at the end of the meeting Jake sensed he had won at least grudging approval from those with whom he was going to work.

Back in his office, Jake plopped down in his chair, loosened his tie, and put up his feet. "You know, I've always wondered what it would be like to argue before the United States Supreme Court. I have a feeling if I have to do that, it's going to be a piece of cake after having done this."

"You did okay, Jake," said Mike. "Nothing used to piss me off more when I was with the FBI than having some other agency honcho simply ignore some threat assessment we had done or some idea we had come up with because it wasn't one of their own. Don't get me wrong, it's not gonna be easy keeping all these guys in line, and there are gonna be people stepping on other people's toes, but hopefully, as far as the heads of these agencies go, you'll be able to work with them and keep them in line."

"Mike, all I know is my job is to get this treaty signed and make sure the President is safe. I will do whatever it takes. If I have to kiss ass, if I have to beg and plead, or if I have to call Jason Bates and threaten to get someone fired, that's what I'm going to do."

Mike looked at Jake and smiled. "You know, I can see you makin' the call to Jason Bates, but I can't see you kissin' ass or gettin' on your knees."

"Very funny. Let's get to work. We've got three and a half months and a hell of a lot to do."

CHAPTER 10

Benjamin Matthews stood at the sink in his jail cell, looking at his reflection in the cracked mirror, and smiled. He patted his face with cold water and wiped it with a semi-clean towel from the hook beside the sink. He went and sat on his bunk and waited while his breakfast was brought in. The same meal as always: powdered eggs, bacon, toast, and coffee. Black pepper, no salt, and the morning paper. He actually liked solitary confinement. He had no desire to be involved with the general prison population. After all, he was not a criminal—he was a patriot. People like Fletcher and Sullivan, the jurors, and that idiot judge in Miami didn't understand. They were among the bleeding hearts who worried about a few people who got hurt when he was trying to save the whole. He could feel his jaw beginning to clench, and he willed himself to calm down. He knew who his friends were and who his enemies were—even here in this grotesque place.

Matthews scanned the front page of the paper, set it aside. He opened the pepper packets, sprinkled them on his eggs, and began to eat. Slowly, he felt himself becoming uncomfortably warm. A flush spread over his face. He began screaming and knocked the tray to the ground, cursing Jordan Fletcher and Jake Sullivan to anyone who was within hearing range, decrying the injustice of him being in prison and the idiocy of entering into a treaty with Cuba. He began pounding the walls, picked up the tray and smashed it against the mirror above the sink, breaking it into small pieces, and throwing himself against the cell door. He grabbed at his collar, which he always kept neatly buttoned, and tore it open, clawing at his throat. He couldn't breathe. His pupils began to dilate and the ache spread from his chest into his arms and down his legs. His knees buckled and he fell to the floor. He began to sweat profusely and his skin became cold and clammy. Keys clanked in the door and someone yelled "Code blue—get the doc in here." Then, someone was pushing on his chest, and then, everything went black.

Jake Sullivan was sitting at his desk when Eva came in, bringing him a cup of coffee. "Jake, did you hear about the latest hurricane?"

"What are we up to now, Eva? I can't keep track of the names."

"This one's called Henry. There's been so many this year, but most of them fizzled out as tropical storms. But this one's made it to hurricane strength, just like that one Caroline did before it headed north."

"Eva, you look worried, not like you to have hurricane jitters."

"Jake, they're saying this one might hit the Keys. I still have a little bit of family there and a whole lot of friends. If that island takes a direct hit from a major hurricane, I don't think there'd be a hell of a lot left."

"Well, they're not sure which way it's gonna go, Eva. It could turn out to…"

"Do you miss it, Jake? Do you miss your friends and the way things were down in Key West?"

Jake sipped some of his coffee and looked at Eva. "I do, Eva. I miss a lot of things. I miss Key West. I miss the people, my friends… but I only ended up in Key West because of the bad things that happened in Miami, many that were my fault, and I caused trouble in the Keys too."

"That's not true, Jake. You know it was Matthews."

"Part of it was Matthews, true. Matthews set me up, but I gave him an easy target. I hurt my family and I still don't have them back. And a lot of good people died. Trouble is, Eva, when I think about Key West, I have to think about all of it. But hey, if you need time to go see your family, and make sure everything's okay, you know you can take it."

"Thanks, Jake. I appreciate that, but I think I'll just stay here. I'm probably worrying about nothing. It will probably go somewhere else. I just hope that wherever it goes, it doesn't hurt a lot of people."

"If you do go, make sure you're out of there before anything happens. You're one part of Key West I don't want to lose."

Closing the door behind her, she stopped and smiled before heading back to work.

Not two minutes later, Eva burst back in the office with Mike Lang beside her.

"Jake, turn on the TV! You've got to see this!"

"What? Did the storm hit?"

"Forget the storm! Turn on the TV! Put on one of the news stations."

Jake did. There was a ribbon going across the bottom and Jake saw it before he heard any of the words. He jumped out of his seat, his coffee spilled on the desk, and he didn't even notice. Scrolling across the television screen in big block letters were the words: DISGRACED FORMER ATTORNEY GENERAL BENJAMIN N. MATTHEWS DEAD OF A HEART ATTACK.

Eva's quick retort snapped his attention back. "Heart attack? I didn't think that miserable bastard had a heart."

Mike Lang started the laughter. Whether it was all the tension surrounding the treaty signing, their combined hatred for Benjamin Matthews, or just the fact that they were three friends who had been through a lot together over Matthews, they couldn't stop laughing. Jake, in an effort to recapture some solemnity said, "Okay, okay, we've got to have a little respect for the dead here."

Mike just shook his head. "Not me. He sure as hell didn't have any respect for us when he was alive. The thing that pisses me off the most is the son-of-a-bitch doesn't get to spend his life in prison. It's an easy out."

They listened to the commentary for a while, which went through the fact that Matthews was going to be buried in the family plot outside of Providence, Rhode Island, and that he had no living relatives, to which Mike interjected, "And no friends, either." Jason Bates appeared on the screen offering the official statement from President Fletcher.

"Without question, the President of the United States does not rejoice in the death of anyone. Benjamin Matthews committed grievous crimes against this country for which he was justly punished. He will now have to make his peace with his maker. The office of the President will have no further comment."

Mike, again, "Why's he so sure he's going to meet his maker and not the other guy?" Eva, clipped him on the shoulder, and Jake just lowered his head and chuckled.

"All right, I guess that's the end of the story, folks. Let's get back to work."

After Eva and Mike left, Jake sat back in his chair, put his hands behind his head, and thought about the whole situation concerning Benjamin Matthews. Could it be true that it was finally over, he thought. It was at that moment that Jake knew there was one more thing he had to do.

He grabbed his coat from the back of his chair. On his way out he said, "Eva, I have to run an errand. I'll be back. I have my cell phone with me. If anything comes up or anyone needs to contact me, just give me a call."

And with that, he was gone.

Jake got out of his car and approached the doorway to Mac's. Even though he hadn't been here since the Matthews' affair, it felt familiar and comfortable. Looking in, he didn't know if this was a good idea, but he knew what he had to do and he stepped inside. Given the time of day, there weren't many customers, and Mac, the owner and bartender, saw Jake as soon as he passed through the door.

"Jake Sullivan. Good to see you, my friend," said Mac, coming over and extending his hand, which Jake shook readily.

"Good to see you, too, Mac."

"Well," said Mac, "To what do I owe this honor, son?"

"Mac, I'm sorry. I should have come back and spoken to you sooner, after everything that happened, but ... "

"No, no, Jake. No need to apologize. I want to thank you for the service you did the country gettin' rid of that crazy bastard, who will now have to answer to the Father Almighty."

"I have to tell you, Mac, there's some dispute back at my office as to whether he's going to have that opportunity."

Mac laughed out loud and said, "That may well be true! But even tortured souls like Matthews probably get a quick peek through the pearly gates before they're sent on their way. How've you been Jake?"

"I've been good Mac. Everything's okay."

"Wife and kids?"

"Let's just say it's a work in progress"

Mac shook his head knowingly. "What can I do for you?"

"Actually, Mac, I want a Corona."

Mac set down the towel with which he'd been wiping the bar and stared at Jake, but didn't say anything. He walked down to the cooler, opened it, pulled out a bottle, flipped off the cap, and sat it down in front of Jake.

"Still no lime, I presume?"

"You're right, Mac."

Mac looked at Jake a little while longer and then said, "I have some business I have to attend to—finish stockin' up for the day. You mind if I leave you here?"

"No, Mac. That's fine."

"I'll be back and we'll talk later."

"Sounds good."

The relationship between a drinker and his drink of choice is a difficult one for people who don't drink to understand. It is many-faceted. Jake closely examined the bottle sitting in front of him. From the moment Mac popped the cap off and sat the bottle down in front of him, Jake could look at nothing else. To a drinker, a bar is something akin to a temple and the drink becomes the chalice from which he gets whatever it is he is seeking. Jake saw the cool wisp rise from the neck of the cold bottle as the vapor met the warm air of the bar. He saw the circles forming in the neck, and he reached out to touch the condensation on the outside of the ice-cold bottle. He picked it up and looked at it. The amber color changed constantly as the bottle reflected the various lights from the bar, and Jake sat there knowing how desperately he wanted to drink that bottle down. Jake wasn't quite sure why he had come here, but he knew that the whole Matthews matter wasn't going to be finished until he did. Mac's was like a lodestone. Jake was at Mac's when the evidence was stolen from his car. Jake's meeting with Steve Townsend was at Mac's. His decision to move to Key West was made at Mac's. The attempts on his life orchestrated by Matthews and his men, his killing of Ortiz, and he and Mike's takedown of Matthews with the help of President Fletcher, had all started because of that desperate need for him to grab one more for the road. And now he knew he didn't have to, and set the bottle back on the bar.

After a brief time, Mac came back, leaned both of his beefy forearms on the bar and looked at Jake.

"What do you want me to do with this, my friend?"

"Mac, I don't think Corona is my drink of choice, so you're probably goin' to have to flush it down the drain."

"My pleasure, Jake."

And with that, Mac took the bottle and emptied it into the sink.

Jake began to put a few dollars down on the bar and Mac walked up to him and put his hand on top of Jake's.

"No counselor. This one's on me. You did it, son. You defeated both monsters; Matthews, the one you didn't create, and this one that you did. And let me tell you, son, it's over. You're fine."

Jake grasped Mac's hand again and shook it.

"Thanks Mac. You've never steered me wrong. I don't know when I'll be back."

"That's all right. You come back any time you want to, Jake."

Jake laughed, "Have a few ice-cold Diet Cokes on hand."

"With pleasure, Jake. With pleasure. Go on out there and keep gettin' the bad guys."

"I'll try, Mac," said Jake. "See ya."

"Hey, Jake," Mac called out to him. "What's it like bein' best buddies with the President?"

"You too, Mac?"

"It's only what I hear, Jake, only what I hear."

As he walked out into the sunlight, Jake recalled that comfortable feeling of sitting and drinking cold beer after cold beer on a warm summer day in a dark, cold bar and then walking out into the sunlight. Today's was even better.

CHAPTER 11

Rain came in from the ocean on the July morning when Benjamin Matthews was buried in a cemetery outside of Providence, Rhode Island. No friends and no family appeared. There was no ceremony. There was no flag. The casket was handled by the employees of the cemetery and it was lowered into the ground without fanfare. Later in the day, a lone taxi slowed as it passed the gravesite, pausing only briefly. The bald man in the rear of the taxi told the driver to move on. He had a plane to catch for an important meeting.

That night, the encrypted password worked its magic again, and a stream of intelligence data found its way into the federal system, worming its way into the threat assessment files of the Secret Service.

Early the next morning, Jonathan Clark e-mailed Thomas Burke, the Head of the Secret Service, that he was going to follow up on a threat assessment he believed had the potential to be a Category IV threat.

AUGUST

CHAPTER 12

Tom Burke, the Head of the Secret Service, which now, technically, was part of Homeland Security, sat at his desk awaiting his next appointment, and he showed all the characteristics of a man who was going to take great pleasure in having a rather heated discussion with whomever that next appointment might be. Just then, his intercom went off. He listened and curtly said, "Send him in," and slammed the button.

Jonathan Clark walked through the door. "Well, look who's checking in. How nice of you, Agent Clark. Where in the hell did you get the idea that you could go dark for almost an entire month and only report into this office with sporadic e-mails as to your whereabouts and what the hell you were doing?"

"Tom, I know. I know you're upset. I know it's not standard procedure, but will you give me a minute and let me explain to you what I found out?"

"You mean you're actually going to be kind enough to share information with the Director of this Agency?"

"Tom, listen will ya? Just hear me out and you'll know why I did what I did."

"All right, Clark. This better be good."

"The morning I sent you the e-mail telling you that I thought there was a serious threat . . . that I was going to check it out . . . was because *this* came through threat assessment and hit my desk the night before."

Clark pulled a printout of an email from a folder he was carrying and handed it to Burke. Burke glanced at it and looked back at Clark. There was a new seriousness in his voice and demeanor. "Go on."

"As you can see, that email contains the code words for both the President and the Castro brothers relative to anything having to do with the treaty signing ceremony. That is highly classified information, only a few people in a limited number of agencies have those code words at the present time.

Tom, you know how any agency within the government or any outside agency, such as Interpol or a foreign intelligence service, has a digital password that allows them to enter raw intelligence. Once it's in the system, guys like me do the analysis and come up with a threat assessment. But we always know where it comes from."

"You're tellin' me some unknown source put data into our threat assessment system?"

"That's exactly what I'm tellin' you. But it is worse than that. Whoever it is also seems to be able to access classified information that should be out of reach."

"So, what you are telling me Clark is that our system is completely compromised?"

"*Was* completely compromised, Tom. When the tech guys gave me their assessment, they also told me they could set up a firewall solely for this digital password so it no longer could get into the system. Before I left for Mexico, I personally supervised the creation of that firewall. Whoever this person is or whatever group he represents isn't getting into the system again."

"That's a small comfort," murmured Burke.

"There's more," Clark explained. "Just last year the system was modified to allow us to determine not only who was entering data, but the location of the data entry. With what was going on with the intelligence agencies in Pakistan and Afghanistan, we were trying to be exactly sure who we were getting information from and where they were. So the tech guys came up with a method to trace back, in half the time something like this would normally take, data to its entry point. Then, for instance, if something came from a region that was controlled by the Taliban, we'd have second thoughts about whether the data we were getting was accurate or not.

That entry point modification was made system-wide, meaning any data entry can be traced back to its source. In this case, it took the guys some time, because evidently whoever did this was pretty smart and bounced his signal from server to server to server all over the world, but eventually they isolated it to an internet café just outside of Acapulco in Baja, California, and that's why I headed to Mexico."

"Jesus Christ, Clark! Do we have any idea how much intel this guy had access to and how many times the system was breached?"

"We're trying to trace back and determine how he established a digital password. We do know that this was the only entry into the system from this unknown source. I did a system-wide check myself, and this information that came through threat assessment was the only entry for this digital password."

"You said it led you to Mexico. What did you find?"

"In Mexico, nothing. But, a source I've used there on other matters dealing with the drug cartels informed me that there's been word of a new Cuban splinter group that calls itself . . . wait a minute, let me check here." Clark shuffled through the papers on his lap. He said, "The name they're hearing is 'The Birth of New

Madrid'. If you look at the signature block on that e-mail, the only things there are initials. B-N-M. I went from Mexico to Miami."

"Clark, you still haven't explained to me why you didn't check in."

"Look, Tom, I didn't know what I was getting into. I didn't know who knew about this. I didn't know whether we had a mole in the government, and I still don't know for sure what's going on. But, I think I've pinned this group down to being a Cuban faction operating in Miami. My sources there tell me there have been rumors of a new group, anti-Castro, and also anti-United States, but pro-Havana, whatever that means. And more importantly, there seems to be a great deal of influence from Spain."

"Spain? What the hell do they have to do with this?"

"I don't know Tom. We need to get people involved with this who know something about these Cuban splinter groups and see what information we can get. But given the fact that they have the code words for both the President and the Castro brothers, I believe we have a viable threat out there that we have to act on."

"Clark, I'm gonna tell you something. My worry is that you have something here. So, we're gonna act on this, but I don't want you going dark on me again. The next time an operation happens, I want to know what's going on—even if you have to find a way to only talk directly to me. I don't want you out there for a month on your own again. Do we understand each other?"

"Tom, like I said, I'm sorry. It won't happen again, but given the urgency of the moment, it was something I felt I had to act on."

"Well, let's hope to hell it turns out to be nothing." And with that, Burke dialed the White House.

Jason Bates, the President's Chief of Staff, suggested a meeting of all the security services in Washington based upon the information contained in the threat. He would pull in everyone he thought should be there and confirm the coordination with Jake Sullivan in Miami.

After the arrangements were made, Burke hung up. "All right, Clark. The White House is taking it seriously, too. We've got a meeting scheduled in two days. Get all your information together. See if you can find out anything else, and be ready to brief everybody on what you found."

CHAPTER 13

No sooner had Jason Bates hung up with Tom Burke than he was on the phone with Jake Sullivan.

"Jake, this is Jason at the White House. I think we have a problem."

"Why, what's going on?"

"I just got a call from Tom Burke, the head of the Secret Service, indicating one of his agents has come across what he believes is a viable threat against the President and the Castro brothers. I've talked to the President and we've ordered a meeting of all the security agencies on Wednesday here in Washington, and I want you to be here. Burke's agent is going to brief everybody on what he's found out, and I have a meeting scheduled tomorrow with a specialist in Cuban affairs to try and get some understanding of what appears to be a new threat."

"What are you talking about, Jason?"

"Jake, as you know, the President has always been a friend of the Cuban population in Miami. He's always gotten the majority of their votes, and their response to the treaty was nothing less than ecstatic. But, based upon the information that Burke gave me, it appears there's a faction that we don't know about that, for some reason, thinks this treaty is harmful to its interests, and it may well be planning to sabotage the treaty signing ceremony or harm the President and the Castro brothers."

"Good god!," said Jake. "That's one factor we thought we'd didn't have to worry about."

"I know, Jake. I know. That's why this thing is so important and why we're taking it seriously. I don't have any other answers for you. All I know is we have to get to the bottom of this, and we're going to. I've talked to the President, and he wants you in Washington on Wednesday."

Jake sighed and thought about his already overcrowded schedule and said, "I'll be there. Do you mind if I bring Mike Lang along with me?"

"I don't care who you bring. Just be here first thing Wednesday morning."

And with that, the line went dead. Jake looked at the phone for a moment, hung up, and called out to Mike.

"Mike, we have to plan a trip."

Lang stuck his head in the door. "I hope we're going someplace nice where it's peaceful and quite."

"Oh, we are. Washington, D. C."

"Do I dare ask why?"

"Let's just say there might be a lead on some party-poopers. Have your bags packed and be ready to go Wednesday morning. I'll explain everything then."

"Aye, aye, captain" he said, retracting his head.

Jake sat at his desk, looking out the window. He had hoped that he could get through this without any major problems. The whole thing was a pain in the ass, but so far, it had been manageable. That the threat level to the President of the United States, or the President of Cuba and his brother had escalated from hypothetical to potential made him very uncomfortable. He hoped against hope that the threat would prove to be nothing, just like all the rest so far.

CHAPTER 14

Their plane landed in Washington at 7:00 a.m. Jake tapped Mike on the leg to wake him up.

"Let's go. Naptime is over."

Lang stretched and yawned.

"So soon? I was just getting comfortable."

"Mike, I think anything having to do with comfort is going to be over for us, at least through the end of October."

Mike looked at Jake and smiled. "You know, you're becoming quite a pessimist as you get older."

"I'm becoming quite a realist as I get older." Mike got up mumbling. "Unfortunately, those two are usually the same thing." He yanked his bag from the overhead and followed Jake off the plane.

Jake had briefed Mike about the meeting and the threat that the Secret Service Agent had picked up. He had also told him about the possibility that this involved a Cuban splinter group. Mike didn't tell Jake anything, but that fact didn't completely bother him. He hoped that the meeting would include a person whom he knew to be one of the foremost specialists on the subject, a person he hadn't seen for a very long time.

The conference room at the White House was full. The heads of the various intelligence agencies that Jake had been meeting with were there, and he had come to have a working relationship with all of them. There were hellos and nods and handshakes throughout the group, and Jake noticed everyone seemed to be a little bit on edge. This was the first true threat assessment they had dealt with throughout their project, and no one yet could predict the severity.

Just as Mike and Jake took their seats, they were back on their feet as Jason Bates led in Jordan Fletcher, the President of the United States. A chorus of "Good morning, Mr. President" was met with "Sit down, gentlemen. Let's skip the formalities for the time being. Jason, let's begin."

Jason Bates, the President's Chief of Staff, began.

"Gentlemen, we believe we have uncovered a new, significant and unexpected threat to the treaty signing ceremony, the President, the President of Cuba, and his brother. I say unexpected because the analysis we have conducted would indicate that this threat is coming from within the Cuban community, which this treaty is designed to benefit."

Jake saw the sideways glances going around the room as members of the agencies sat up and took notice. Then James Kirkland, the head of the CIA, spoke up.

"Wait a minute, Jason. There has never been any animosity in the Cuban community toward the President. I understand how they feel about the Castros, but this treaty gets rid of the Castros and gives them their country back. Why would they try and sabotage it, and more importantly, why would they try and harm the President?"

"Jim, that was our question, too," said Bates. "But we've had an in-depth analysis of this situation done, and I think you'll find that there's every reason to consider this a credible threat.

I suggest we let Tom Burke present the information that was discovered by members of his Agency, which would seem to indicate that there's been a serious breach of classified information, as well as an unauthorized entry of intelligence data into our system. I think Tom can best explain the protocols that have been taken to prevent all further access and what the threat entails. Once he's finished and we are no longer discussing classified information, you will hear from a Cuban analyst we have been working with who will make this whole picture much clearer.

Tom, why don't you begin? You all know Tom Burke. Tom, fill us in on what you found out and what's going on."

"Jason... Mr. President... I'd like to give the floor to my agent, Jonathan Clark. He's the person who discovered the threat, and he would like to brief everyone on what he's found."

"That's fine, Tom," said Bates. "Mr. Clark, you have the floor."

"Thank you, Mr. Bates. Mr. President. Approximately a month ago, the threat assessment files received a data entry, the source of which appeared to be outside of Acapulco in Baja California, Mexico. The entry consisted of one sentence. You'll see a copy of the data entry in your briefing books. As you can see, it states, 'The Hawk and Doves will soar but then be consumed in the pit of Hell.'

There are very few people outside of this room who know that *Hawk* is this operation's code word for the President of the United States and *Doves* is the word for Fidel and Raul Castro. I went to Mexico to see if I could determine anything from the location of the data entry, but I came up blank. I did, however, find out from my sources in Mexico, who had gotten confirmation from sources in Miami, that there appears to be a new Cuban splinter group strongly influenced by Spain that calls itself 'The Birth of New Madrid'. If you look at the data entry, there are initials on the bottom after the one sentence entry. Those initials are B-N-M, which I believe stand for 'Birth of New Madrid'. My sources in

Miami confirmed that they've heard rumors of a new group out there which appears to be both anti-Castro and anti-United States, which I will agree, based upon all our prior information doesn't seem to make much sense. If you're anti-Castro, especially in this situation, it would seem you would support the treaty, and want to see it signed, which would also seem to indicate a pro-U. S. stance. But, anti-Castro-anti-U. S. is what my sources in Miami are indicating to me is out there. We don't know whether this message is a threat, a tip from someone that a threat exists, a hoax by some hacker, or anything else at the present time, but that's the information we have so far and I believe it constitutes a credible threat.

Additionally, we have ensured that the system can no longer be compromised, as our tech group has created a firewall, which will prohibit this unauthorized digital password from gaining access to any information and from entering any further data into the system. We believe any further ability to gain any type of access to the system has been neutralized."

Jake Sullivan had been watching Clark's presentation, and it was odd. He sensed something familiar about the man but couldn't quite place it. He shook his head. He had been through so many meetings, listening to so many reports from so many sources, he realized Clark really didn't sound that different from anyone else.

Jason Bates once again rose to his feet. "Thank you, Mr. Clark, for your presentation. Thank you also for your efforts in uncovering the existence of this unauthorized breach of our security systems and your quick action in determining its potential source and in preventing further breaches.

Gentlemen, unless there are specific questions and/or comments you feel you need to make at the present time, I would like to bring in the analyst on Cuban affairs who, hopefully, will put the information that Mr. Clark has obtained into perspective. Understand that the analyst in question does not have clearance for certain aspects of our discussion and has only been provided with the information we believe necessary to allow her to analyze the possibility and probability of a threat against the President from the Cuban community. Accordingly, I would ask that you be cautious should you feel the need to ask questions or make comments as to this presentation."

With that, Bates turned to a guard at the door. "Please show her in."

The door opened and a beautiful, dark-haired young lady entered the room.

CHAPTER 15

Mike Lang, who had been leaning back in his chair with his hands behind his head sat bolt upright and stared at the doorway. Jake noticed the smile forming on his lips and looked from the young woman to Mike and back again.

"Someone you know, Mike?"

Mike nodded slightly. "You could say that."

This caused Jake to smile himself.

Jason Bates then announced the new arrival. "Gentlemen, may I please introduce Paula Cortez. Ms. Cortez is a Cuban specialist with the FBI, knows the history of the region and all the various groups we've been dealing with, both anti-Castro and pro-Castro, and other groups who might have anything to do with our situation. I've asked her to give us a briefing on just what this situation might involve. Ms. Cortez."

"Thank you Mr. Bates. Mr. President. Gentlemen. I've had the opportunity to review the portion of an alleged communiqué from a Cuban splinter group. I must start by telling you that up until this point in time we have not heard of a group that goes by 'Birth of New Madrid'. However, I've read Mr. Clark's briefing paper and it is not farfetched to assume that this does deal with a Cuban splinter group heavily influenced, not by Spain, but by Cuban Spaniards."

With that, the Secretary of Homeland Security spoke out. "Cuban Spaniards? What do you mean by Cuban Spaniards?"

"I think it would be helpful if I gave you a brief history lesson. You have to understand that at one time Cuba and Havana constituted the spearhead of Spain's attempt to carve an empire out of the New World. In 1634, King Philip of Spain designated Havana by royal decree 'Key to the New World and Rampart of the West Indies'. All the Spanish treasure ships that left the New World gathered in Havana before setting sail across the Atlantic. When those ships were in the port of Havana, Cuba, it was the wealthiest city in the world. There has always been an undercurrent throughout the Caribbean among Spanish speaking people and those of Spanish descent to re-establish some type of alliance, some type of 'Spanish empire in the New World', or 'New Spain', or possibly 'New Madrid'. It is conceivable that a group has formed that sees this treaty as a potential annexation of Havana and Cuba to the U.S. and, therefore, the ultimate destruction of those dreams. You have to realize that the great opposition against Castro when he took over in Cuba wasn't from the Cuban peasantry. They loved him. They thought he was going to bring them utopia. His opposition was from the entrenched... wealthy... elite. Gentlemen, that elite class in Cuba were those who had come to Cuba from Spain. At the time Castro took over, twenty-five percent of the Cuban population was either those who had come from Spain or their descendants and they held the positions of power that Castro took away. There is no question that those people would have a deep-seated hatred for Fidel Castro and his brother, Raul. But as I said, it is also conceivable that they have a deep-seated opposition to this treaty. I think that we haven't seen this splinter group before because the United States was never a threat to the wealthy Spanish elite. Both wanted Castro gone. But this treaty is a game changer. It brings Cuba into the United States' sphere of influence and will not allow it to stand independent and alone as it was before Castro, undermining this group's dream of a greater Spain. I think it is absolutely essential that this threat be considered viable. Thank you."

It was quiet around the room as the agency heads looked at one another, trying to figure out what they were going to do next. President Fletcher sensed the disarray and spoke.

"All right, gentlemen, here is what we do. We carry on as we have been. This treaty signing is going to happen and nothing is going to prevent it, and it's going to take place at the end of October, when we said it was going to take place. I will notify Raul Castro and his brother of the situation and make sure they understand that we are doing everything possible to thwart this threat and ask them to ensure that their intelligence agencies are cooperative with us in providing us with any information that they discover. Jake, I want you to concentrate on this in the Miami area. See what you can find out, see what type of threat this might be, how it might be carried out . . . anything you can find, and I want it stopped. Are we clear, gentlemen?"

"Yes, Mr. President."

"Very well. Thank you." And with that, President Fletcher and Jason Bates left the room.

People sat somewhat stunned by the information, none more so than Jake Sullivan, who now had the hunt for a potential assassin or assassins placed directly in his lap. As always, Mike Lang broke the ice.

"Seems to make the whole thing more exciting, doesn't it?"

There was some nervous laughter around the table and Jake rose and spoke. "All right, gentlemen. Let's keep things going as we have been. Obviously, this is the top priority. Anybody hears anything, I want to hear about it one second after you do. Use all your sources, all your resources. We're in August. We have a little under three months left. We need to identify what the threat is.

Once we do that, we'll know how to extinguish it. And gentlemen, we will extinguish it. Neither the President of the United States, nor the Castro brothers, are going to suffer harm in my city. Are we understood?"

There were general nods of approval, and Jake sensed he was finally in charge of this group, a position he certainly didn't relish, but one he was determined to carry out.

Just as Jake and Mike made their way out the door, ready to leave, Paula Cortez came up to them.

"How are you, Agent Lang? Or I should say, former Agent Lang? Now a private citizen, I believe?"

"Paula, it's good to see you. How've you been?"

"I've been fine, thank you, fine."

"Paula, this is . . ."

"I know who this is, Mike. Mr. Sullivan, it's a pleasure. I've heard a lot about you and your escapades involving Benjamin Matthews, who has since had the decency to make sure we do not hear from him again."

"Ms. Cortez, nice to meet you. That was quite a presentation you put on in there."

"Just doin' my job."

"Yeah, she's really good at doin' that," said Mike.

"I take it you two know each other," said Jake.

Mike spoke up first.

"Yeah, when I first started with the Bureau here in Miami, Paula was sent down to help me with some Cuban gangs that were forming, using the Cuban Freedom Organization as a cover. She was very helpful."

"Thank you, Mike. Yes, that was back in the days when Mike and I both worked for the Bureau, but now that he's elevated himself to one of the President's best friends, he's gone and left us all behind."

"Paula, ease up, would you? The sarcasm dripping on my sleeve is making it a little wet."

"Mike, I'm just kidding. You know that. I'm happy for you. I'm glad you're doing so well."

"And by the way," said Mike, "I don't think I'm one of the President's best friends." He looked at Jake. "Am I?"

Jake just shook his head. "I have to admit, Ms. Cortez..."

"Please call me Paula."

"Paula... that I've heard that more than once lately and I think our relationship is being somewhat exaggerated."

"All I can tell you, Mr. Sullivan..."

"Please... Jake."

"Very well. All I can tell you Jake is that the word at the Bureau is that you're the President's man in Miami, and as Mike appears to be your chief sidekick, I'm assuming that he's up there, too."

"Paula, I have to be getting back to the office. Mike, let me have a word with you alone, please, and then take your time coming back. Please, reacquaint yourself with Paula here, and then I'll see you later today."

Jake took Mike aside. "What exactly was your relationship?"

"Let's just say we worked closely together for a while... very closely."

"And what happened?"

"She went back to Washington and I stayed in Miami, and whoever said that absence makes the heart grow fonder is full of shit."

"She meet someone else at the Bureau?"

"Worse. Her college professor in Spanish languages at Georgetown."

"She dumped you, an FBI agent, for a college professor?"

"Yeah. Thanks for rubbin' it in. I know."

"All right. Listen, she seems interested enough. Give it a shot. See what happens."

"Jake, are you actually giving me romantic advice?"

Jake just laughed. "Yeah, I suppose you have a point there, but ahh... take your time. I'll see you at the airport later. Our plane doesn't leave for a while. Just make sure you catch up with me before it does."

"Thanks."

Jake started to walk away.

Mike said, "Hey, by the way."

"What?"

"I really don't think of myself as your sidekick."

"Get back there and play nice, Tonto."

Mike started to laugh. "Yes, Kemo Sabe."

Mike moved back inside the doorway, hoping that Paula would still be there, and sure enough, she was.

"Sorry, Paula. There were some things we had to work out before Jake headed to the airport."

"No problem, Mike. I'm used to you pushing me aside for work."

"Wait a minute Paula. Let's back up a little bit. If I recall, it was you who left Miami to go back to Washington."

"And I certainly couldn't convince you to come with me."

"Paula, I was just starting out in Miami. I liked it there. If you remember, I asked you to stay."

"Mike, you know I had the inside track to a good position at the Bureau's main headquarters. How could I give that up?"

"Look, Paula, let's not argue, okay? We each had to do what we had to do. You went back to Washington and I accepted it. By the way, how's the professor at Georgetown doing?"

"Long gone."

"Really?"

"Yeah, it was funny. The wife that he told me he didn't have became very upset when she found out about us. The last I saw him he was picking his stuff off the yard in front of my apartment as I threw it out the window."

Mike didn't say anything, but just smiled.

"And don't you stand there and smile. And don't you dare tell me that you told me so."

"Not a word, Paula. Not a word. Listen, I have to catch up with Jake. Our plane's gonna take off to head back to Miami."

"Good. I'll walk with you."

"Why? Where are you headed?"

"Same plane. I've been assigned to Miami 'til this thing's over. Given the Cuban/Spanish influence involved, they think I can be a help to Jake and you down there."

"Well, we're glad to have you on the team."

"Yeah, I'll bet."

And with that, Paula walked out in front of him, leaving Mike standing there. The only thing he could think of was, "Here we go again!"

CHAPTER 16

It had rained the night before and the hollow situated in Harlan County, Kentucky, was damp and the humidity hung in the air. The six men sitting around the dilapidated porch of the shanty waited for the arrival of their guests. One side of the porch was covered with the Confederate battle flag, while the other had a Nazi Swastika hanging from the rafters. An older man, heavy set with a beard, spoke to the others.

"Boys, we gotta make sure our buyers aren't no undercover feds. We're gonna do some serious checkin'. Make sure these boys have a clean bill of health b'fore anything changes hands or anything's talked about. We're gonna check for wires. We're gonna check IDs. We're gonna send Jonas inside on the computer to run those IDs—make sure exactly who it is we're dealin' with. These boys are buyin' a heavy load of shit. They mean to do some serious damage some-where or they're settin' us up. Either way, I'm makin' sure that this deal goes down without no problems. We understood?"

There was a murmur of assent among the men seated around the porch.

"Good, 'cause here they all come."

Two black SUVs with tinted windows were coming up the rural road to the shanty. The six men on the porch, all of whom were armed, loaded their magazines, took the safeties off their weapons, and stood, their weapons pointed downward but in the general direction of the SUVs. Their leader got off the porch, but only to the first step. Thinking himself a military tactician, he remembered reading that you always meet the opposition on higher ground. The fact that he was six foot two and weighed three hundred pounds and was standing about five feet off the ground should do the trick.

Four men got out of each SUV. Two moved toward the steps while the others remained just outside their doors.

"Gentlemen, welcome to Harlan, Kentucky."

One man stepped forward, obviously the leader of the group from the SUVs. He had a noticeable scar on his face and his blonde hair was cut close to his head. Dressed in camo with a Sam Brown belt around his middle, he was lean and strong, clearly former military.

Had the leader of the men on the porch truly been a military tactician, he would have noticed the other six men moved slowly away from the doors of the trucks in a fanning motion so that all of them would have clear sight lines to the group on the porch.

The leader of the SUVs spoke.

"It is my understanding that you have some material that we need."

From the top of the step, the leader of the porch spit a wad of tobacco to the ground at the other man's feet.

"Who you boys been talkin' to that gave you that information?"

"Does it matter?"

"Yeah, it matters. It matters a whole hell of a lot. Boys."

And with that, the group on the porch raised their weapons slightly, pointing them at the leader of the SUVs.

"Not a very friendly welcome, my friend."

"Well, ya know, my momma told me be very careful in dealin' with strangers. And you boys are definitely strangers. Now, here's what's gonna happen. You and your boys are gonna stand real still while my men frisk you all for weapons, and you're gonna provide us with IDs and we're gonna check those IDs, and you are gonna tell me where you heard about us. And if all that goes well, then I believe we can do some serious business, as long as you brought some serious money."

The leader of the SUVs stood perfectly still. His eyes never left the leader of the porch. He stood like that for what seemed an eternity and finally, the leader of the porch, impatient, yelled out, "Well, what's it gonna be?!"

Without raising his voice, the leader of the SUVs slowly shook his head and said, "I don't think so." An instant later, a fully loaded Glock materialized in his right hand. He fired, hitting the leader on the porch through his right eye. At that same instant, the six strategically placed men who had been in the SUVs fired, and within seconds, the other five men on the porch were dead, none of them having even gotten off a shot.

With that, the leader of the SUVs walked up the steps and kicked the leader of the porch off the step to the ground. "Stupid fuckin' hillbillies." And he proceeded into the shanty.

They emerged carrying two boxes of C-4 plastic explosives, loaded them into the back of the SUVs, backed out of the path to the shanty, and were out of Kentucky heading east within an hour.

A local paper in Harlan County reported the following week that six family members had been gunned down in their shanty, the inside had all the makings of a meth lab, and the murders were believed to have been part of the ongoing meth wars for which Harlan County had become famous.

CHAPTER 17

Jake Sullivan sat at his desk and rubbed his eyes. It was early morning. He had just finished his second cup of coffee. He had spent the night at the office, sleeping on the couch. He picked up the morning paper, glanced at it, and threw it back on his desk. The news cycle about the upcoming treaty signing was starting to intensify. He looked at the phone messages on his desk from more reporters than he cared to think about wanting information and interviews, none of which was going to happen. The only other item of any interest was the newest report of the latest tropical storm forming out in the Atlantic.

"Just fuckin' great," thought Jake. "I have a treaty signing with the Presidents of two countries in attendance, I have some crazy group running around who wants to kill 'em both for which we have no leads, and I never know when a goddamn hurricane is gonna strike the place where the treaty is gonna be signed. Shit, could it get any better?"

At least Eva was relieved. Hurricane Henry had just grazed the Florida Keys and not caused any damage in Key West. Unfortunately, it pounded the Yucatan Peninsula mercilessly, causing over five hundred deaths and millions in property damage. The other storms that had formed petered out and no other major hurricanes were reported, but there was some concern about the newest one forming, and if it did, in what direction it was going to head.

Just then, there was a knock on the door and Jim Nelson, an Assistant Prosecuting Attorney, stuck his head in.

"Jake, can I pick your brain?"

"You can pick what there is of it. This morning I'm not sure there's too much left."

"C'mon Jake. It can't be that bad."

"How'd you like to take over this job Jim?"

"Huh! No thanks boss! Hey, remember, no guts no glory."

"Yeah, I'll remember that."

"Listen, Jake, do you remember having a case back before..."

"It's all right, Jim. Back before I got fired and went to Key West? Is that what you're trying to say?"

"Yeah, Jake, I'm sorry. But, yes, back then. Do you recall the securities fraud case we were doin' where the guy skipped with about $25 million in negotiable instruments, and as far as we got was trackin' him to Mexico where we thought he had some type of plastic surgery?"

"Yeah, I remember the guy."

"Wasn't there somethin' odd about the surgery?"

Jake thought back. "Yeah, supposedly there was some guy in Mexico that had perfected some new miracle type of plastic surgery. With this technique, he could make you into a completely new person and your scars would heal in less than a month, based upon the technology he was using. We could never prove the guy existed. He had some weird nickname... Dr.... ummm... Dr.... Dr. Invisible, and the tracks of the guy who skipped ended in Mexico. As far as I know, we haven't found anything since."

"Well, I don't know if it means anything and I don't know if it will help the case or bring it back to life, but I wanted you to know we just got some information over the wire that the Federales raided an estate in Acapulco. They thought it was a distribution point for one of the drug cartels. They raid the place and they're in the barn and they find a secret trap door in the floor under the hay. They go down, and this is what they find."

With that, Nelson laid out a group of pictures.

"Holy hell," said Jake.

"I know. Look. It's a complete modern operating theater. The thing is, apparently, none of the plastic surgeons these guys have talked to recognize any of this equipment. They say it's all completely new... off the charts... something they've never seen, but it appears that its purpose was plastic surgery. And the Federales also found this..."

The picture showed a middle-aged man in a white lab coat sitting in a chair with his hands tied behind his back with a single gunshot wound to his forehead. There were pictures of the chair taken from all angles, showing his hands tied, his head laying off to one side, and a front view clearly showing the shot.

"I don't know, Jake," said Nelson, "this guy could be our Dr. Invisible."

"Yeah, well, it looks like somebody didn't like his work or someone wanted to make sure he couldn't talk about his last surgery."

"His name is Simone Lorenza, a former doctor in Mexico City who lost his license through some insurance scam. Anyway, I just wanted to let you know we got this and I'll keep you posted if we turn up anything about our missing 25-millionaire guy. Hang in there with this other stuff, Jake. You'll take care of it."

"Huh... yeah. Thanks for the vote of confidence, Jim. I appreciate it. I hope the hell you're right."

That night there was another entry in the threat assessment data bank. The technicians were on alert, but they were focused on the previous means of entry, and this one was routed in a completely different manner and came in along the route normally reserved for data received from Interpol and other foreign intelligence agencies. The coding ensured that the information would remain hidden in the files for two more weeks and then be routed to threat assessment at the Secret Service Agency.

SEPTEMBER

CHAPTER 18

Jonathan Clark stood in the shower under the hot water for a long time and thought about his day. The information he had obtained, which he would present at his meeting with Sullivan would produce the first big break in the case and he was excited. Seeing how Sullivan worked and working so close to him, was a thing of beauty. And when he dropped this bombshell in Sullivan's lap, it was going to be spectacular. Clark got out of the shower and dried himself, dressed in the clothes he had gotten ready, and made sure everything was as it should be as he stared in the mirror. He took another gulp of coffee, left his half-filled cup on the kitchen counter, checked himself once again in the mirror, and was out the door, whistling a tune as he went down the steps.

CHAPTER 19

The young lady working behind the counter in the art supply shop in Georgetown found nothing unusual about the man who entered her store asking if she might have some items he was looking for. Other than walking with a slight limp, he had the look and the mannerisms of an artist. His voice had a slight tone of superiority, but didn't they all? He had longish hair, a goatee, and seemed to know exactly what he wanted. She took him to an area that had the items he might be interested in and he quickly made his selection, thanked her, paid cash, and was out the door. Her only thought was her hope that she would have more customers who decided so quickly and paid in cash so easily throughout the rest of her day.

In a similar fashion, the elderly lady at the Department of Public Records took no notice of the construction worker who entered her offices approximately an hour later with a request for two documents—the printouts for all the buildings fronting Collins Avenue in the vicinity of North Shore Park. He seemed very pleased with the detail in the plans—heights, access points, all methods of entry and exit, windows, and other information was clearly available. He was just as pleased when he reviewed the second plan he had asked for, which seemed to provide the detail and information he was looking for. He thanked her very kindly for her assistance and didn't seem bothered when she reminded him he had to sign for the plans and presented him with the book for his signature. She almost thought his smile turned to a sneer as he looked at her, but she must have been mistaken because he quickly signed, smiled broadly, and thanked her once again for all her help.

CHAPTER 20

Jake and Mike were busy going over the details of the arrival times of the President and the Castro brothers when the intercom sounded. It was Eva.

"Jake, Jonathan Clark's here. Says he has some information that's urgent."

"Show him in, Eva."

Clark came in and went directly to Jake and Mike, standing at the conference table. Just at that moment, another man entered the office, noticed Clark, smiled, went up to him, and extended his hand.

"Hey Jonathan, how've you been?"

Clark had to calm himself and tone down his excitement at the information he was about to give Jake and Mike. He looked intently and quietly at the man whose hand was extended before him. Finally, he broke into a large smile, recognizing the man before him as Dave Thomas, a member of the Secret Service from the Washington Office.

"Dave Thomas, how are you?"

"Good Jonathan. Hell, I've been hearing some amazing things about you. You go dark for a whole month and a half and come up with this… with all this information about this plot. You're becomin' a legend at the Agency."

"Hey, just doin' the job. Got a tip, followed it through, got lucky on some information provided to us, and here we are. Why are you here, Dave?"

"Ah, Burke sent me down with some information for Mr. Sullivan here. Monthly reports detailing all the info we got in August. Unfortunately, there doesn't seem to be much we can hang our hat on."

"Did you get that new data that just came in from Interpol?"

"What are you talking about Clark," said Jake, "What information?"

"Jake, you're not going to like this, but I have to tell you what happened. Somehow a couple weeks ago we had information sent to us from Interpol about a known assassin who just might be our guy."

"Two weeks ago? Why the hell are we getting it now?"

"I don't know what happened, Jake. There was some kind of glitch in the routing system. It clearly shows that data was entered into our system two weeks ago, but for some reason it didn't route and appear until yesterday."

Jake threw some papers across the room.

"That's just fuckin' great! We have information of a potential assassin we could have been working on for two weeks, now here we are in September and we're just getting it?"

"Jake, calm down," said Mike, "Clark's here. Let's hear what he has to tell us."

"I'm sorry, Clark. This just pisses me off. Go ahead, what's the information?" said Sullivan.

"This deals with an assassin who goes by the code name 'The Agent'. Evidently, Interpol's been tracking his movements and they think they placed him flying out of Paris several weeks ago, destination unknown."

Mike spoke up.

"So we don't know if he's here in Miami or not?"

"There's more," said Clark. "This guy's been a suspect in several assassinations with ties to Al-Qaeda terrorists, the KGB, and most importantly, to Cuba Libre, a prominent free Cuba group. My sources indicate to me that there was a sighting of this guy in Havana last week boarding a flight to Miami."

"So what you're tellin' me," said Jake, "is that this guy potentially has been here in Miami for a week, doing whatever he has to do to get ready to assassinate the President of the United States, the President of Cuba, and his brother?"

"It looks that way, Jake."

"Jesus Christ! We have anything else? Any way we think we can find this guy?"

"There's some more information. This guy's weapon of choice appears to be an AS-50. That's a 50 caliber 12/7 mm sniper anti-material rifle."

Mike whistled. "Jake, he could take out the whole podium and anyone near it with that thing."

"Interpol indicates that the guy walks with a pronounced limp and he uses numerous disguises, but his favorite seems to be posing as some type of artist. Seems to favor carrying an easel case, and that's where he conceals his weapon while he's moving about."

"Anything else?" said Jake.

"No, but look. I'm going to go down into Little Havana. I figure if this guy's working with someone in Miami, it has to be someone in the Cuban population, given how this whole thing's playing out. I'm going to see if any of my sources have anything that indicates someone's seen anybody that even remotely looks like this guy or could be this guy. If so, we will see if we can track him down. If he's here, Jake, we'll find him."

Jake was staring out the window shaking his head.

"We damn well better find him." He then turned and looked at Clark. "Go ahead, Clark. Get out on the street. See what you can find."

Clark turned and looked at Jake before he left.

"Jake, sorry about the delay."

"Yeah, yeah. I know. I know. It's over with. Just go out and find this guy."

"Don't worry, Jake. We'll find him," and Clark left.

"Yeah," muttered Jake. "Don't worry... right."

Jake looked over at Mike, who was sitting there deep in thought.

"What's the matter Mike? Something bothering you?"

"Yeah, there is something bothering'me." Mike looked at Jake, and then walked into the next conference room and handed out the information from Clark. Then he asked the security team gathered there, "Anybody ever hear of this guy? All of a sudden, this assassin appears out of the blue with all this information about him. How come we never heard about this guy before? And why is there so much known about him?"

Jake looked over at Mike and said, "Mike, how many times have you dealt with Interpol in a matter that involves an international assassin?"

"Me personally? Never. But how about the rest of the guys in the room? Homeland Security, did you ever hear anything about this assassin?"

Jess O'Donnell, their liaison with Homeland Security spoke up, "No, Mike, but in all honesty, unless there's a viable threat against the country, we really wouldn't have."

"I don't know," said Mike, "It just doesn't seem to make sense to me."

"Look, Mike," said Jake, "Look at the Jackal."

"The Jackal?" said Mike.

"Yeah. You heard of the Jackal, the famous assassin."

"Sure, everybody has. Hell, there's been books and movies about him."

"That's my point. The guy was still functioning as an assassin and the media knew all about him. They knew he was born in Venezuela. They knew his real name, Illich Rameriz Sanchez. They had photographs of him. And still, Carlos the Jackal was a legend, 'till he finally got caught for killing those guards in France and is now serving life in a French prison. The fact that there's information on this guy doesn't make him any less credible a threat."

"I know. I know you're right. There's just something odd about it to me," said Mike, "I don't know what it is, but there's something odd."

"Well, at least this gives us something to go on," said Jake. "It gives us someone to look for and find and maybe end this threat against the President and the Castro brothers. Thomas, when you go back, make sure you tell Burke about this development. Thomas, you listening to me?"

"Yeah, yeah, Mr. Sullivan. I'm sorry. I was just thinking about Clark."

"What?"

"Well, you know, Clark's not a guy that's usually full of surprises. Clark's by the book and by the numbers all the time. Him going dark . . . it just seems out of character for him and then he's wearing his gun on his right hip."

"What's odd about that?" asked Mike.

"Well, when Clark joined the Agency, he put down in his records that he was ambidextrous, but we've known each other for a while and he confided in me that he's really left-handed. He put down ambidextrous because he felt that as a lefty there might be some prejudice against him getting a good position with the Agency. However, knowing Clark, he practiced, and became as proficient with the right arm as he was with the left because that's just the way he is. But he always wore his gun on his left hip. Just now he had his gun on his right hip. It just threw me for a minute. Don't worry, Mr. Sullivan, I'll give a full report of what's going on here and I'll send you a copy of the information so if there's anything you want to add, you can follow through with Director Burke."

"All right, Thomas, thanks," said Jake.

And with that, the meeting ended.

CHAPTER 21

It had taken several months. Fall had come. The word had finally come. Eduardo Rivera had waited patiently. Another note had been dropped in his cell last night. His freedom, his reward, and his life back in Mexico were waiting for him. As he left his cell, he looked around at the hellhole and spit on the ground. Then, he followed the same route to the kitchen that he'd taken on the night he had gone to find the pepper packets.

The kitchen was dark as he entered. He was told to wait there. Someone would meet him to provide him with clothes, money, and an escort out of the prison. He sat on one of the kitchen chairs and waited.

He found his thoughts drifting to Mexico... the house, the cars, the drugs, the women.

It was in the middle of his reverie that he heard a noise behind him, but he never had a chance to turn. The arm around his throat was huge. As he looked down, he recognized the tattoos of the Aryan Brotherhood, just as he felt the knife enter his back. As the life rushed out of him, he couldn't decide which he would miss most, the house, the cars, the drugs, or the women, but it really didn't matter.

OCTOBER

CHAPTER 22

The sky was as blue as could be, but the wind was blowing strongly and the waves were pounding against the beach. The Coast Guard ships on their picket line were bobbing up and down. Tropical storm Louise was brewing in the Atlantic and though it appeared to have turned north, some of the computer models had it doing another turn, bringing it back toward Miami. It was a storm of immense proportions, with the outer bands being some five hundred miles from the eye, and even if it progressed up the coast, there was significant risk of torrential rains and winds in the Miami area.

Jake had received word from the White House to keep things moving. The storm would be dealt with if it had to be but, otherwise, the treaty signing was going to go through.

Jake couldn't help but think that the fates were playing games with him. Not only did he have to deal with one of the most powerful human forces on earth, the President of the United States, but he also had to deal with one of Mother Nature's most powerful forces, a potential Grade IV hurricane.

The term "hurricane" is the name given to tropical cyclones that form in the western hemisphere that exceed the intensities of tropical depressions and tropical storms. Storms that meet the same criteria that form outside of the Atlantic Ocean and northern Pacific Ocean, east of the International Dateline, are normally referred to as cyclones or typhoons, depending upon the area in which they form.

According to the Saffir-Simpson Hurricane Wind Scale, a Category IV hurricane has wind speeds in the range of 131 to 155 miles per hour, a potential storm surge of 13 to 18 feet, and the ability to cause widespread coastal destruction and erosion. It is the next to highest category rated. The devastation to the Miami area, if such a category storm hit, would be unimaginable.

They were only a few days away from the treaty signing and there was still no sign of their assassin or any new information on the 'Birth of New Madrid'. They talked over the details about the podium placement, seating, and security, following the sight lines from the various buildings along Collins Avenue, which would be unoccupied and protected by multiple security forces. They went over the schedule of the helicopter fly-overs and the Coast Guard ships carrying Seal teams.

"Jake, what the hell are we going to do if this storm does hit?"

"I don't know, Mike. It's not our call. We're supposed to move forward with everything. I guess it will be a last minute decision for the White House."

"Do they understand that it's going to be impossible to set all this stuff up if the wind's worse than it is now?"

"Mike, what can I tell you? I have my orders from the White House."

"Typical bureaucrats," mumbled Mike. "They never listen to the boots on the ground."

Just at that moment, Mike's cell phone rang and he moved off, trying to position himself in the ever-increasing wind so he could hear the call. After several moments, he returned.

"Jake, that was the Coast Guard Station down in Key West. One of their cutters on patrol in the Florida Straits picked up three Cuban refugees trying to make their way to the United States."

"And?" said Jake.

"And, they all had Spanish passports. I think I should go down and find out what's going on."

Jake thought about it for a moment and said, "Yeah, do that. And take Paula with you. Her knowledge could be a help given the Spanish passports."

"I'll call her and we'll be on our way," said Mike, and he turned to walk away. But just then, a mischievous smile crossed his face. Knowing full well how much Jake loved his BMW Z4 convertible, but also knowing how well it would serve his purpose on this particular trip, Mike quietly asked, "And do you think I could borrow your car?"

Jake looked at Mike and smiled.

"Son, you wouldn't be going out on a date, would you?"

"Jake, don't give me any bullshit. Can I use the car or not?"

"May I ask why?"

"If I have to drive down to Key West anyway, it seems like a nice day to do it in a convertible."

"Would this be especially true, given your passenger?"

"Jake..."

"It's all right, Mike. It's all right," and he threw him the keys. "You and Paula have a good time, and take care of my car. Just keep your cell phone on so I can get you if I need you, and keep me posted on what you learn."

"I will, absolutely. And you know, I can be back from Key West in an hour and a half or so."

"Mike, depending upon what you find out from the Coast Guard, I don't need to see you until 9:00 a.m. tomorrow, right here. But if I do call you, you better get your ass here as fast as you can."

"Hey, it's your car."

"Mike . . ."

"I know. Just kidding boss, just kidding. Thanks Jake. I appreciate this."

Mike had walked some distance away from Jake when he stopped, turned, and looked back at him. Jake was looking out to the ocean and Mike walked back.

"Jake, you sure you don't need me to stay?"

Jake never turned around.

"Mike, it's okay. Go. I'll call you if I need you."

Mike turned, walked away, but stopped again abruptly.

"You're not gonna bust my balls and call me every five minutes, are you?"

Jake just turned around and looked at him, smiled, and started heading for the northern end of the park. Mike shook his head and headed for Jake's car.

CHAPTER 23

Tropical weather is a funny thing. Although a major storm was brewing somewhere out in the Atlantic not far off the coast of the Florida Keys, the weather on Mike and Paula's drive down had been beautiful. The sky was blue with wispy clouds and it stayed that way until they pulled into Key West in the early afternoon.

As soon as Mike hit Key West, he made the right onto Roosevelt Boulevard, went over the Palm Avenue Causeway, took a left on Eaton, and a right on Grinnell, and made his way to Trumbo Road and the United States Coast Guard Sector Key West.

There, he and Paula were met by Command Master Chief Petty Officer Carnell Gooden. Mike took one look at the Chief, who stood six foot five of solid muscle. The firmness of his hand-shake and the look of his eyes, set in a face the color of smooth milk chocolate, led Mike to believe he was dealing with a man who took his job very seriously.

The depth of the investigation that Chief Gooden had already conducted affirmed Mike's suspicions.

"The story I got from these three through an interpreter," began Gooden, "is that they had traveled to Cuba from Spain on some type of school field trip, and one of them, thinking he was pretty cute, started making speeches that weren't too flattering to

Castro. Unfortunately, he did it in public, and Cuba being Cuba, the next thing he knew he and his buddies were snatched up by one of Castro's goon squads and were taken in for interrogation. Since then, their parents in Spain have been trying frantically to get them off the island, but they're tied up in the red tape that Cuba uses when they really don't want someone to leave.

Hell, the oldest one of them was only nineteen. They've been locked up with some hard-cores, and they're scared to death.

So, then they get word that Castro's planning one final purge before the treaty goes through and these guys, who are under some type of modified house arrest in the hostel where they were staying, get the bright idea that they're going to escape. They put whatever money they had together and somehow found somebody willing to give them a boat, and off they sailed into the Florida Straits. You know how many times I've heard this kind of story before? And usually it ends in tragedy. These guys were lucky. We got to them just outside of Cuba's territorial limit and picked them up, and there was a Cuban patrol boat hot-tailing after them, and they really would have been thick in shit if we hadn't gotten to them first."

Mike spoke up, "Do you buy their story, Chief?"

"Well, here's what I did. I called their parents in Spain and talked to them. What these guys are telling plays out with what the parents say. I had them fax me some information about the kids and checked on their names through all the databases. They come up clean... parents' stories make sense. Personally, I think they're three scared kids who won't shoot off their mouths too much anymore when they're in a strange place."

Paula spoke up, "Chief, do you mind if we talk to them?"

"Nope. I was already faxed documentation from Homeland Security. You have full access."

"Paula, why don't you go in there and talk to them? See if you can pick up anything. I want to go over these documents the Chief has and the summaries of his conversations with the parents and these boys to see if I can pick out anything. When you're done, we'll sit down with the Chief and see what we think."

Forty-five minutes later, Paula came back out the door and Mike had just closed the file. They asked one of the guards on duty to go get the Chief, who joined them five minutes later.

"Paula, tell us what you think."

"I think the Chief's right. Those are just three scared kids in there. All they want to do is go back to Spain. They don't want to stay in Key West. They don't want to go to Miami. They want to go home. I tried dropping every clue I could without telling them why we were here. There was no recognition whatsoever. I looked for every tell that I know that would indicate they were lying and I didn't see it."

"I agree with her, Chief. I watched part of her questioning through the two-way and I couldn't pick up anything either, and I've done this quite a bit. I think your analysis is dead on."

"So, what should we do?"

"Are the parents willing to pay for their flights back?" asked Mike.

"Absolutely," said the Chief.

"Let's get them on a plane out of here. From the sound of things, they've been punished enough for being a little bit stupid."

That brought the first smile to the Chief's face.

"You sign the authorization?"

"You get it ready and I'll sign it," said Mike.

A half hour later, Mike and Paula watched from their car in the parking lot as three now-smiling young Spanish men were put into a Coast Guard van, headed to the Key West Airport, then on to Charlotte, North Carolina, New York, and home.

Watching them go, Paula said, "I know they were wrong, but I feel sorry for those kids."

"Look at it as a learning experience," said Mike. "I have to call Jake. I'll be back in a minute."

Mike got out of the car and walked a distance away and hit Jake on speed dial.

"Well, how are things in the Garden of Eden?" asked Jake.

"Nothing here, Jake," said Mike. "Turned out to be three kids who were bustin' Castro's balls and he didn't like it. He had them rounded up. They decided flight was their only recourse. But they're clean Jake. We went over everything. There's nothing to it. I put them on a plane back to Spain."

"You're sure?" asked Jake.

"Absolutely," said Mike. "If there was even a hint, I would have brought them home for further questioning, but there's nothing to it. If we're giving out merit badges when this thing is all over, you might want to consider one for a Chief Petty Officer down here named Gooden. He did a nice job on this one."

"I'll make a note," said Jake.

"All right, we're heading back."

"Mike, I already gave you your orders. I don't want to see you until 9:00 o'clock tomorrow morning. Understood?"

"Jake, are you sure..."

"Mike, quit asking me. I'll see you tomorrow."

And with that, the line went dead. Mike walked back to the car and got in.

"What did he have to say?"

"My good friend and wonderful boss just gave us the rest of the day to enjoy Key West. You've never been here, right? Well then, allow me to show you the sights."

Paula sat back, smiling from ear to ear, as Mike got on Eaton and headed in to Old Town.

Mike took Paula to the Schooner Wharf Bar to listen to the last few songs of Michael McCloud, who performed there every afternoon. Sitting at a table under one of the canopies they laughed and talked, watched the tourists and the Key West regulars, and watched the dogs getting their food out of the hole cut in the kitchen wall.

After eating way too many peel-and-eat shrimp, Mike told Paula they were going to go for a walk. They headed out on the wooden decking of the Historic Seaport Boardwalk around the various shops and restaurants. Off in the distance, Mike pointed out where the proposed ferry terminal was going to be when traffic started again between Key West and Cuba, a dream for so long but now poised to become real.

But this was not the time to talk about the treaty signing, or the President, or the Castros, 'The Agent', or anything else. Mike took Paula down Front Street, crossed Duval and headed back to Mallory Square.

As with everything else in Key West, Mallory Square had a long and storied history. Legend has it that it was once the chosen anchorage for pirates and later the anti-pirate campaigns orchestrated by Commodore Porter in the 1800's. It had been the center of the wrecking industry that led to great fortunes in the city of Key West.

While the story is that Tennessee Williams was the first person to initiate the ritual of applauding the sunset at Mallory Square with a gin and tonic firmly in his hand, it appears that what has become known as the Sunset Celebration really began in the 1960's, when groups of hippies descended upon Key West and Mallory Pier in search of their own version of paradise. About thirty to forty regulars high on LSD used to come down to watch the sun drop into the Gulf and, gradually, it became a celebration encompassing the whole community. In the late 1970s and early 1980s, more and more vendors came to sell their wares on the dock at sunset, and the city fathers were renovating the dock to accommodate cruise ships. When merchants adjacent to Mallory Square began complaining about the unsupervised event, the city of Key West determined that something had to be done.

In typical Key West fashion, realizing the irony in having government intervention in a sunset, an individual who was arrested for selling art on the pier at sunset, several vendors and performers, and the world renowned Cookie Lady formed a legal entity known as the Key West Cultural Preservation Society, Inc., in 1984. This organization created guidelines for the sunset celebration and actually negotiated a lease with the city of Key West so that sunset could "be managed" and the artistic integrity of Mallory Square be preserved. Only in Key West.

Mike moved Paula to the edge of the quay so she could see out into the Gulf, and they sat down on the edge. They watched the *Western Union*, the flagship of Key West, sail past, silhouetted against the setting sun and watched as the red ball continued its slow but steady drop into the sea.

When it was over, Paula looked at Mike with amazement in her eyes and said, "Mike, that was truly one of the most beautiful things I've ever seen. Thank you for bringing me."

And with that, she gave him a long and deep kiss. As they separated, Mike looked her in the eyes and said, "Paula, the pleasure, absolutely, is all mine."

They smiled and kissed again. Mike said, "C'mon. We're gonna go for a little drive."

"Where to?" asked Paula as she got up.

"Why, the whole way to the Atlantic Ocean, of course."

Smiling again and holding hands, they headed for the car.

Mike drove down Green Street and made a left onto Whitehead, pointing out Ernest Hemingway's house, the lighthouse, and finally the red, black, and yellow buoy that marked the "Southernmost Point in the United States."

Mike pulled the car over as they watched couples getting their photographs taken by the locals capitalizing on a good opportunity.

"C'mon, let's go," said Mike.

Laughing, they got out of the car and walked over to stand on either side of the buoy while a bearded man in faded cap and t-shirt agreed to take their photograph for a couple of bucks. Despite attracting legions of tourists, it actually isn't the southernmost point in the United States. Florida's official southernmost point is Ballast Key, a privately owned island just south and west of Key West. Also, during low tides, several sandbars farther south than Ballast Key are exposed, the southernmost of which is Sand Key. Even on the island of Key West, the buoy does not mark the actual southernmost point, which is in the Truman Annex, controlled by the United States Navy and not accessible to civilian tourists. In similar fashion, the private yards directly southeast of the buoy, certain beach areas of Truman Annex, and Fort Zachary Taylor, a historic state park, are all farther south—but who's measuring, this is Key West.

Paula was looking out at the ocean as Mike came up to her.

"Mike, this is an amazing place. It truly is."

"It's one of the best places on Earth as far as I'm concerned. Someday I'm going to end up here or tending bar at the Soggy Dollar."

"What's the Soggy Dollar?"

"It's a little bar on White Bay on Jost Van Dyke, an island in the British Virgin Islands."

"Why's it called the Soggy Dollar?"

"Well the way the ocean floor is there, you have to moor your boat so far out that you either have to swim or take a raft in. Hence, everybody's money usually gets wet . . . hence, the Soggy Dollar."

Paula laughed and said, "And that's your ultimate goal, huh?"

"Don't knock it 'til you've tried it."

Paula nestled up to Mike. "I'd love to try it sometime with you, Mike. I truly would."

"C'mon. I'm gonna take you to a place where the view is even better and the food is out of this world."

"I don't know Mike. It's hard to imagine anything better than what you've showed me so far."

"You shall see, my dear. Let's go."

And with that, they got back in the car. Mike headed down South Street, made a right onto Vernon Avenue, and then the left onto Waddell. He was happy to find a parking place right along the hedges where the road went down to meet the ocean.

"What is this, Mike?"

"That place to your left there . . . it's one of the best restaurants in the world, Louie's Backyard."

Mike led Paula along the side of the building and through the gates to the Afterdeck. Mike was happy to see that most of the tables were open and he chose one right along the railing bordering the Atlantic and went to the bar to get them each a drink.

As he approached, he saw a man sitting at the corner of the bar who resembled a tropical Santa Claus, whom he knew to be Phil Tenny, the owner of Louie's. Mike introduced himself, telling Phil how happy he was to be back. Phil, as gracious as ever, welcomed him and bought them their first round of drinks.

When he arrived back at the table, Paula was sitting with her chin in her hands, gazing out at the Atlantic.

"Well, Paula, what do you think?"

"It's absolutely breathtaking. It's hard to imagine that out there somewhere there's a huge storm growing when it's so beautiful and peaceful right here."

"A lot of the old timers in Key West can actually sense what weather's coming just by looking at the water and smelling the breeze. You know, Jimmy Buffett used to live next door to this place, and he wrote a song about storms forming out on the water. It sort of sums up that the people here take things as they come, weather included, and just go about their business."

"I do notice the wind's picked up a little bit since we've gotten here," said Paula.

"Let's hope that *little* is the operative word and that this thing doesn't come anywhere near Miami."

Neither Paula, nor Mike, could know that the forecasters had been accurate, and as they had begun their drive to Key West the storm actually was well on its way north, heading on a direct path toward New England. It was proceeding at a rapid rate over the relatively warm water of the Atlantic Ocean, growing into an immense storm that would strike in the wee hours of the morning with a devastating force that would have implications reaching the whole way to southern Florida.

"Okay, Mike. Let's not talk about work, the storm, or anything else for a little while."

"I agree," said Mike, lifting his glass in a toast.

"Here's to being at one of the most beautiful places on Earth with a most beautiful lady."

Paula clinked his glass. "Compliment accepted," and she laughed.

They sat there talking and looking out at the ocean for some time and as it got dark, moved up onto the Terrace for dinner. Mike chose the Bahamian conch chowder with bird pepper hot sauce and grilled diver scallops with shrimp cream and trenette in pesto. Paula opted for the heirloom tomatoes with fried fresh mozzarella and basil oil and the sautéed Key West pink shrimp with bacon, mushrooms, and stone-ground grits.

They dined slowly, obviously enjoying each other's company, often touching hands, their conversation interspersed with laughter and lingering looks. When they were done, having refused dessert and finished their last sip of wine, Paula reached over and took Mike's hand.

"Mike, thank you. This was a beautiful day. The food was absolutely amazing and the view—it's unimaginable. I can't believe it took me so long to come here, and I can't wait to come back again."

"That's the way this place is," said Mike. "That's why so many people who come here stay."

"Were you surprised when Jake decided to return to Miami?"

"Paula, you have to understand, Jake was living his dream in Miami before he had to come to Key West. He was like so many people who end up here because they have lost everything else. It has a lot of good memories for him, but some pretty significant bad things happened as well. Mike lost some friends here because of his dealings with Matthews and I know it haunts him."

"Is he any closer to getting back with his wife?"

"They're working on it. Jake's changed. He was always a good man, and he was always dogged in his pursuit of justice... hell of a good attorney. But there's an edge to him he didn't have before. Almost being killed and killing does that to a man. I think Linda sees it, and I think it scares her. She's afraid of what might happen to him because she knows he won't back off. She knows that if he has to get involved in something, he'll see it through, danger or not. She's worried as much for her daughters as anyone. I just hope they can work it out because I know Jake loves her, and I know she loves him, but sometimes that's not enough."

"You know, Mike, that man you described reminds me of someone else I know."

"Not me, I'm trying to avoid all those things."

"Yeah, sure. That's why you were beside Jake every step of the way in putting an end to Matthews, and that's why you're by his side every step of the way on this."

"It's different Paula. First of all, Jake's my best friend. I have to be there. And secondly, I don't have anyone else out there to worry about or to worry about me, so things are a lot less risky for me than they are for him."

"Don't be too sure about that, Mike."

"What?"

Paula leaned across the table and kissed him lightly on the cheek.

Mike smiled just as the waiter came. They declined anything else, Mike paid the bill, and they moved to the car.

"Mike, I apologize but I don't think I'm going to be much help to you. After all this food, I'm afraid you're going to have to do the driving and I'm going to fall asleep in the passenger's seat."

"You know, about that... I was concerned given Key West's reputation that we might over indulge while we were here, so to be on the safe side, I took the liberty of reserving a room at the Pier House Resort in case we decided that it was unsafe for us to drive back to Miami tonight."

Paula stood there and looked at Mike with her hand on her hip and said, "And just how many rooms did you reserve, Mr. Lang?"

Mike looked at the ground and looked back at her.

"One."

Paula smiled as she opened the passenger side door.

"Awful sure of ourselves, aren't we?"

Mike laughed. "You just said I was one to take chances."

"And what does Jake think about all this?"

"I forgot to tell you... he gave us the night off, too."

"Get in the car, Lang." And he did.

They walked into the Pier House and registered. Mike had requested a room on the first floor directly across from where one of the entrances to the Chart Room used to be. Now it was part of an Art Deco foyer since the owner of the Pier House evidently believed that the historical significance of the Chart Room was outweighed by the need for a "re-do" on the hotel lobby. The most ridiculous aspect of the re-do was that if you went into the Chart Room bar from the other entrance, the door and windows were still in place, but now opened only onto an interior plaster wall.

As they entered the foyer, Mike pointed to the left and said, "That's our room. Do you want to go to the Chart Room for a nightcap? Could be a lot of Key West characters in there."

Paula grabbed Mike by the hand and pulled him toward their room. As they came up against the door, she embraced him and kissed him passionately.

"I'm with the only Key West character I want to be with tonight, thank you."

Mike fumbled until he got the key card into the slot and the door clicked open. Wrapped in each other's arms, they practically fell into the room and the door closed behind them.

CHAPTER 24

Jake had to admit as he looked out over the ocean and felt the stiff winds on his face that he was relieved by the whole situation. There were only a few days to go before the ceremony and thank goodness Hurricane Louise had shifted north.

He felt badly for the people of New England, who were bearing the brunt of this gigantic storm, but it was one less thing he had to worry about.

They still hadn't located 'The Agent' but that was a problem created by man that could be solved by man. Louise had been something he had no control over and it now appeared that the storm was not going to be a problem.

Just then, he heard Mike Lang.

"Good morning, Jake. I heard about the weather. Looks like we finally got a break."

Jake turned to see Mike walking across the park, hand in hand with Paula Cortez. Jake smiled as the two of them approached.

"Well, Mike, ready to get to work?"

"Sure, that's why I'm here. I'm always ready to work, you know that."

"I assume things went well in Key West?"

He thought he saw Paula blush as Mike said, "Yeah, everything's fine. And before you ask, your car is back, washed and sparkling in the exact same condition as when I left. Here are the keys."

Jake caught them as they were flipped toward him and smiled.

"Paula, feel free to come along with us. We're going to go over the layout of everything one more time and check all the security details."

"Thanks, Jake."

Jake caught the smile between Mike and Paula and he had to admit it made him think about Linda. He was happy for Mike, but unfortunately, there really was work to do.

"Mike, you sure all those buildings on Collins have been cleared out?"

"Before I left yesterday, Jake, I went over that with the security force that has that detail. They had done a room-by-room search and everybody was gone. Some not too happily, I might add, although things got better when we explained that they were going to be put up in a first-rate hotel at government expense until the treaty signing was over."

"How are we going to keep it updated?" said Jake.

"Roving patrols through every corridor, every hour. All doors are unlocked. First sign of a locked door, the team has a go ahead to bust in. Sniper group up on the roof, the building checked top to bottom the whole way through the basement to the roof."

"All right Mike. Sounds like you have it covered. I want those people reporting to you every hour."

"I'm on it."

"What about the overheads?"

"Helicopter flights continuous up to the actual time of the ceremony. We have to pull them then because the sound will drown out the ceremony, but it will be at the last minute. There's a perimeter setup with fighter planes on standby and helicopters further out so no one can penetrate the airspace. Complete radar lock on the area for a distance of fifty miles. Nothing can approach without being seen."

"What about the park perimeters?"

"As you can see, they are all sealed off tight with orange construction netting, guards every twenty-five yards, only one entry point, metal scanner in place. IDs will be issued the morning of the ceremony to all those invited to attend, and the access code on those IDs will be activated only when the first person arrives for entry. They will be scanned to ensure a match."

"What about those working the perimeter?"

"The actual officers who will be working will be picked at random the morning of. No one has advance knowledge of where they will be. Their IDs will only be issued as they are set in place. That way there can be no advance switching of IDs with anyone, and no one can take the place of anyone in advance because no one will be sure exactly where they're supposed to be positioned or whether they are even going to be on the detail."

There was a flurry of activity in the park as chairs were set up, the podium finalized, and electrical wires were being run everywhere as Jake, Paula, and Mike moved from the north end of the park to the south.

"What about the ocean side?"

"Coast Guard already has their picket line established—complete sonar. Nothing can come under them or through them. There are two Seal teams on two Coast Guard ships ready to move at a moment's notice: one with demolition experts and the other a strike force, of which no one except security is aware."

"Looks like we have it covered," said Jake.

"Jake, I don't see anything else we can do."

"What we can do is find this goddamn assassin. He knows all this is going on. He knows what the difficulty's gonna be, but he's here. That means he has a plan to get through security. He's gonna try it, Mike. I know he's gonna try it, and we have to get to him before he does, because God help us if he succeeds."

They had reached the southern end where some men were unrolling the orange construction netting around posts that had been planted.

"What's this?" asked Jake.

"We don't need any more room than this for the people who are coming, so we're cordoning off the park here, and this will form our perimeter on the southern end."

Jake walked past the posts.

"What's down here to the south?"

"Nothing much. The park ends at the inlet and there's nothing there but a rocky slope down to the water. The Coast Guard has a team checking the beach, including that, every hour."

Just then, Paula cried out and stumbled. Mike turned quickly and caught her as she was about to fall.

"What happened?"

"I think I just broke my toe on something."

"What the hell?"

"What is it?" said Jake.

"Looks like an old grate."

Jake walked over and saw a rectangular metal grate approximately six feet by four feet, somewhat recessed and edged in concrete. But the grass had grown up obscuring the edges, and that is what Paul had stubbed her toe on. It appeared to be hinged on one side and secured on the opposite side by a hasp with an old rusty padlock. If it were opened, the grate would fall inward and hang from its hinges against the wall of a large subterranean drainage canal. It was dark and nothing could be seen, but the sound of lapping water from below was clear.

"What the hell is this, Mike?"

"That inlet that I told you about . . . this used to be the catch basin for Collins Avenue. Water runoff would come down through the drain grates in this park and flow out to the ocean. When they reconfigured Collins, the drainage patterns changed, but this would still work as an overflow. That water you hear now is tidal; when it comes in, the underground chambers fill up, and when it recedes, they empty. Other than that, there's nothing there."

"What's our security on this?"

"Like I said, Jake, the Coast Guard checks the inlet every hour, but with the tide nobody can stay down there, so there's no place an assassin can hide. One of the Seal teams already went in. You can only get in so far. After making your way through a couple twists and turns that the water has cut into the coral, you arrive at a cavern with a large pipe in one wall—it used to carry all the water down into the ocean. Since it's no longer in use, it's been sealed off with a welded metal grate that is still secure. The Seal team tells me it's made of some type of anti-corrosive carbide. Who knew? Anyway, beyond that are numerous pipelines—the old feeder pipes— but they're small and it would be very difficult for a person to fit through them, even if you could even get through the metal grate, and then they completely fill up with water. And trust me, given the weather and the high tides no one could survive being yanked out of those pipes by the suction of that tide going back out if you're there at any time after 9:00 p.m."

Jake thought about it.

"Mike, I know it's outside the perimeter, but to be on the safe side, on the morning of the ceremony I want the Seals to sweep the inlet again, go in and make sure that nothing's been tampered with, and I want a guard posted by this grate. I don't want our boy popping out of here the morning of the ceremony, taking out a guard, blending in with the crowd, and making his way to the President."

"Jake, like I said, I think it's an impossibility, but we'll make sure it's taken care of."

"Good. Paula, you okay?"

"Yeah, just hurt my toe. I think I'm all right."

"What's this over here, Mike?"

"That's an old parking lot no one uses anymore. It's basically abandoned. You can see how the weeds are growing all over. The entrance is through a gate up at the side of the park. We have a car with two security agents parked there at all times."

Jake looked north toward the podium, out toward the ocean, and back again.

"Good job, Mike. You've done nice work here."

This led Paula to give Mike a little squeeze of the hand, which did not go unnoticed by Jake.

He smiled and said, "I don't think there's anything else we can do here. Let's get back to the office and see if we have any more information on our friendly assassin."

CHAPTER 25

That night, a truck slowly pulled into an alley behind one of the many bodegas in Little Havana. Louis Peron had been expecting them.

Two months ago he had been called by a member of Cuba Libre and been told that a shipment was coming that he should store with his other supplies until he received another call and the shipment would be picked up.

Louis's parents had both been imprisoned by Fidel Castro and he was an ardent supporter of the Free Cuba movement. The group had helped him financially in setting up his little restaurant and used it as a meeting place and a place where information could be passed as was needed without interference or prying eyes.

He never knew the source of the calls he received, but he never failed to agree to help in any way that he could. The second call had come yesterday, and he was told that this night the shipment of "moros y cristianos," "black beans and rice," was going to be picked up.

Two men entered the bodega from the alley and he directed them to the boxes. They were quickly loaded into the truck and he closed the door, thinking that once again he had served the cause and maybe even a little reward would come his way.

He never heard the man with blonde hair cut close to his head and a scar on his face re-enter the bodega, and felt nothing as the razor-sharp blade slid across his throat, his assistance to Cuba Libre at an end.

The sea was rough that night, even though the hurricane had moved north, and the men were taking no chances as they scampered along the rocks of the inlet south of North Shore Park. They had timed it to perfection. Coming along the beach farther south, and then fighting the increasing tide and swimming along the shoreline and into the inlet, had taken one-half hour, leaving another half hour to complete their mission within the hour between the Coast Guard's patrols.

All the men were dressed in swimming trunks only, two carrying water-proof backpacks with the equipment they would need. They entered without using any light and slowly made their way through the initial twists and turns of the passageway leading from the sea, trying to avoid the sharp coral outcroppings as they went. Finally, they entered the cavern that was approximately twelve feet high, ten feet wide, and ten feet deep. On the wall directly in front of them was a metal ladder reaching from the floor of the cavern to a large drain grate that was centered in its roof. To their right was a circular metal grate, blocking the circular opening of the pipe. The blonde-haired leader looked at the glowing dials of his watch.

"Tide comes in full strength at 9:00 o'clock. Unless you want to be sucked out to sea, we have one-half hour to get this done. Now move!"

With that, one of the men pulled out a container of an oily compound from his backpack, and smeared some on each of the joints of the bars that formed the metal grate, then he moved out of the way, as another focused a laser beam at each of the bars in succession. The bars immediately began to glow red hot, illuminating the whiteness of the scar on the leader's face as he looked upwards, able to see the stars in the night sky through the drain grate opening directly above him. In less than five minutes, the bars were severed, and he motioned for quiet, even though their efforts so far had been done with the greatest of stealth. Satisfied that there was no one above them, he motioned the men to proceed.

The remaining men had covered themselves in oil. They pulled at the metal grate, and grudgingly it came free. One of the men pulled a black-coated rag from his knapsack and clamped it over the burnt ends of the grate. Each man squeezed into the pipe behind where the grate had been and the last man pulled the grate toward him and put it back into position. With all signs of the burned joints obscured with a black film, even with a flashlight playing on it, no one would be able to tell that the grate had been cut. The men moved quietly, pushing their knapsacks in front of them, following their leader. When they came to a point where all the pipes split off in various directions, without hesitation the leader chose the one to his immediate right and they moved on.

Safely in darkness, the leader pulled out a penlight and looked at the GPS he had taken out of one of the backpacks and whispered to the man behind him, "Hundred and fifty yards to go. Tell the others." Slowly and quietly the word was passed back.

Watching the GPS as he crawled, he reached the point he was looking for. Items from the backpacks were slowly passed from one man to the other until they reached the leader, who unwrapped what appeared to be pencils and blocks of clay with wires running between them. He then took out a timer, entered a code, and pressed the start button. The clock began counting down to detonation time: 1200 hours, October 28. Sealing the entire device in a waterproof pouch, he took a small hand-held battery powered drill and drilled two small holes into the metal surface of the pipe above him. He picked up a metal strap with predrilled holes on each end, and secured the package to the top of the pipe, securely screwing each end to form a bracket that held the device in place. Taking a moment, he looked up, knowing that at noon on the 28th, the Presidents of the United States and Cuba, and Fidel Castro would be standing directly above this location at that time.

It was painstaking work for the men to ease their way backwards out of the pipe system and when they reached the area where the pipes split off, the water was beginning to come up over their heads. The leader halted the group and one of the men with a backpack removed portable breathing devices and masks, which he passed out to members of the team. Donning the masks and turning on the devices, they began moving, now completely under water. They also began to feel the pull of the tide, as moving out of the pipes went much faster than going in.

When they reached the grate, the leader checked his watch. No Coast Guard patrol yet. He gave the signal for the men to wait while he reached through the severed metal grate and attached a metal clip trailing a long nylon cord to the rungs of the ladder that led up to the drain grate in the park. The line was run through metal clips on a nylon belt that each man had put on over his swimming trunks.

When this was done, checking the joints of the grate and ensuring that nothing had been tampered with, the leader once again signaled for his men to wait, pushed the grate open, and immediately was pulled out toward the inlet. It had been his choice to assume the dangerous role of first one out, as he would not have the benefit of the line he was going to secure at the opening of the inlet. As he was pulled through the opening, he elongated his body, hands fully in front of him to make as narrow a target for rock outcroppings as possible. Fortunately, the tide was not yet at full strength as they had planned, and he made it to the opening with only a few minor bruises.

Emerging from the water and scurrying up the incline that led up to the park, he secured the rope around a large coral outcrop and pulled it taught. He then gave several strong pulls on the rope, the signal to the other men to move out. While their leader had been making his way through the passage, the remaining men had struggled with the tide, and ensured that the metal grate had been wedged back into place. The oily compound they had placed on the severed edges was impervious to sea water; nothing would seem amiss to anyone inspecting the cavern.

Having received the signal from their leader, the men released themselves to the pull of the tide. In single file, they crawled down the rope hand over hand, feet first toward the inlet, using only their strength and the rope line to keep them from being sucked out into open water.

When the team reassembled, the lead man silently moved the men back into the ocean, where they swam quietly along the edge of the coast to the south, fighting the ever increasing tide until they were once again safely on the beach, their mission completed.

Ensigns Kosior and Taylor were sitting at their sonar screens that night and observed nothing unusual. The only thing that appeared were the usual schools of fish moving up and down the coastline.

CHAPTER 26

Carlos Perez was sitting in an apartment and couldn't believe his good fortune. Just a day ago he was homeless. Having had his leg crushed in a work injury several years ago and being unable to support himself, he had learned to live on the streets.

But that was when the man had approached him. He was nothing out of the ordinary—appeared to be a construction worker—but he told him he was planning a surprise birthday party for one of his best friends and had rented an apartment where they were going to hold the big party, and explained how he wanted the surprise to happen.

He'd had a bath and a shave, had his photo taken, and $500 stuffed in his pocket. Now, all he had to do was sit here in this apartment, and when the front door opened, yell "Happy Birthday," and fire what he had been told was a toy gun into the air.

He looked around the apartment. It was basically bare. An easel had been set up alongside a box with some sort of art supplies, and a long tube lay against the window ledge. There were some papers lying around and a laptop computer on a desk. There was a mattress on the floor with a pillow and a blanket and some canned foods on a shelf.

Carlos thought it strange, given the fact that this was to be the site of a party, but maybe his benefactor had rented it from the guy who lived here who could only afford the basics.

Carlos wondered how much he would get if he tried to fence the computer and the other stuff, but he figured he better not push his luck. The $500 was feeling mighty good in his pocket. Nope, the best thing he could do was to wait for that door to open, and that's what he was going to do.

CHAPTER 27

Jake was walking up and down in front of the large board they had constructed with all the information, the leads they had received about the 'Birth of New Madrid' and 'The Agent'. Jake paced back and forth trying to find something... anything that he had missed that could give him a lead.

Clark was at a desk working the phones trying to get information, and Mike was on the phone going over the last minute details with all the security forces. The ceremony was the day after tomorrow and they still had no leads on the assassin.

Jake looked at Mike, who just shook his head, meaning there was nothing new. Jake slammed his fist on his desk in exasperation and reached to take another swig of coffee when he heard Clark.

"What? Where? Tell me exactly where you saw him. Give me the description again. You sure? Yeah, I know. I know the description is on the flyer, I know. Yeah. Yeah. You'll get the reward, if it pans out. But I'm tellin' ya what, if you're jerkin' us around, I'm comin' down there after you, you understand me?"

Clark slammed down the phone and looked up. Jake and Mike were both looking at him.

"Well?" Mike said, "What?"

"Look, you know how many responses we've had to the flyers we posted that haven't panned out, like that girl at the art store that said someone matching the description of our guy with a limp had come in to buy art supplies, but we couldn't get any further with it than that. This guy that just called is usually a pretty good source. He tells me he spotted a guy goin' into an upstairs apartment in Little Havana. Said he walks with a limp. Said he was carryin' a bunch of artist stuff. He said he thinks he saw the same guy go into the apartment a little while ago, and he hasn't seen him come out."

"We have the address?"

"Got it."

"Let's go. Mike, get the teams together and we'll meet you there. C'mon Clark, you're driving."

He threw Clark the keys to his government car. Clark reached across his body and snagged them with his right hand and did two quick little slaps on his desk with his left.

"This might be it, Jake, this might be it."

"Christ, let's hope so."

The teams had quietly entered the streets of Little Havana and surrounded all entrances and exits of the apartment building in question. Quietly, Jake, Mike, and Clark led the assault team up the steps to the apartment where their suspect was supposed to be. Jake looked at Mike and nodded. Mike gave the go ahead to the SWAT team member carrying the battering ram, as he hit the door it caved in. Mike and Clark entered first with Jake right behind them.

The man seated in the chair before them jumped up and fired a shot. His words were drowned out by his gunfire and the gunfire from Clark's weapon as he placed two rounds in the man's chest. The man they hoped was 'The Agent', their assassin, lay before them dead.

CHAPTER 28

Clark was in his office filling out final reports when Jake came in.

"Nice work, Clark," and Jake reached out and shook his hand.

"Pleasure's all mine," said Clark, "Thank God we got the guy."

"Yeah, just in the nick of time," said Jake. "The President and the Castros will be flying in tomorrow and the ceremony is the next day."

"Jake, listen, I gotta run. I gotta get this info off to Tom Burke and see what he wants me to do next. I'm catching a flight out of Miami for Washington in an hour, so I'm heading to the airport. Give Mike my best, and I'll probably be back down here for the actual ceremony."

"I hope you can make it back, Clark," said Jake.

"I wouldn't miss it. It's always good to get the bad guys and have justice prevail."

And with that, he was out the door.

Jake was sitting at the desk when Mike came in.

"We got back the analysis on that laptop we found. It shows the purchasing of the airline tickets in Paris to Havana to Miami, has coded entries for bank accounts in the Cayman Islands that we haven't been able to get into yet, but it looks like there was recently a large deposit. We're tracking down the numbers and should have that info soon. That tube that was by the window with the artist easel had an AS-50 in it. We also did an analysis on those papers we found. Looks like this guy definitely had a connection to the 'Birth of New Madrid', had been down in Havana, and probably, based on what we can tell, got to Miami about a month ago. He matches all the known descriptions of 'The Agent' that we have. I guess we got our guy."

"I'll start alerting all the members of the team and all the protective units and get a hold of Jason Bates. What's the matter, Mike? You don't look convinced."

"It's that same feeling I had before, Jake. Something about this was just too easy."

"Easy? Mike, we had nothing on this guy. If Clark's source hadn't come through, we might never have found him. We've been looking for him for at least a month, and we just get him in the nick of time, and you think that's easy?"

"I know, Jake, I know. I can't tell you what it is. There's just something bothering me. Hell, you're right, we should be happy. Looks like we escaped two disasters. We got this guy and we missed the hurricane. Did you see what that thing did to the coast in New England?"

Hurricane Louise had slammed into the New England coast early in the morning, causing widespread damage and death. Reports were still coming in, but it looked like one of the worst natural disasters suffered by that part of the country in some time.

Just then, the phone rang. Jake answered it.

"What? Why does he want to talk to me? What? All right, hold on. Mike, I'm gonna put this on speaker. Listen to this. Hello, this is Jake Sullivan."

"Hello, Mr. Sullivan, this is Carl Monroe. I don't know if you're the guy I'm supposed to be talkin' to, but I wanted to pass on some information I thought might be important."

It was hard not to notice the New England twang in Mr. Monroe's voice.

"Go ahead, Mr. Monroe."

"I'm the caretaker up here at St. Ann's Cemetery just outside of Providence. You are that guy that was involved with that mess with Benjamin Matthews when he was Attorney General, aren't you?"

"Yes, I am. Go on Mr. Monroe."

"Yeah, well I've been tryin' to get a hold of somebody. Phone service is really bad up here given the storm that hit. Pretty well wiped us out you know. Whole town's gone along the coast."

"I'm very sorry to hear that Mr. Monroe, but could you get to the point of why you're calling me?"

"Well, it's a funny thing. Our cemetery's right along the coastline. When that storm came in, it washed out a lot of the gravesites here, and one of them was where your Benjamin Matthews was buried. Took his casket and rolled it right over—half opened it. Well, we've had a lot of folks buried here washed out to sea, and I ain't sayin' that couldn't be what happened to him, but it looked to me when that casket was laying there open that part of it was filled with rocks. Again, I can't tell you what happened, but it just seemed odd to me and I just thought I should let somebody know. I called the local authorities and they gave me another number to call, and eventually someone suggested that I call you, so they transferred me and that's what I did."

Jake looked at Mike, and Mike could see the alarm on Jake's face.

"Mr. Monroe, thank you very much for your call. We'll look into it. I'm sorry for what you've lost up there, and I hope everything turns around quickly for you."

"Thanks. I appreciate that. We'll work hard to get everything back to the way it should be. We've had these storms before. We're used to them."

"All right, Mr. Monroe, take care," and Jake hung up the phone.

Jake walked over and stared hard at the board where all their evidence was located, turned around, and looked at Mike.

"Jake, you don't really think . . ."

"I don't know what to think," Jake said, and started pacing back and forth.

"Jake, the bastard's probably just been washed out to sea."

"But what about the rocks?" Jake said, continuing to pace back and forth in the room. Time and time again he walked past the board, staring at the evidence that they had pinned.

"Jake, what is it? What's bothering you?"

Finally, Jake slammed his fist down on the desk.

"That son of a bitch! It's him!"

"Jake, what are you talkin' about?"

"It's Matthews! This whole goddamn thing is Matthews!"

"Jake, have you lost your mind? What the hell are you talkin' about? He's dead."

"The hell he is," said Jake.

He grabbed a marker off his desk and went over to the board.

"You remember that banner that ran across the TV screen the morning we heard about Matthews' heart attack? Do you remember what it said?"

"Yeah, it said the son of a bitch had died of a heart attack."

"It said, 'Disgraced former Attorney General Benjamin N. Matthews, dead of a heart attack.'"

"Okay, Jake, so I don't have your power of total recall. What's the point?"

"The point is his name," and Jake moved to where they had posted the information on the 'Birth of New Madrid' and he circled the B and the N and the M.

"Benjamin... N... Matthews... Birth of New Madrid. This goddamned egomaniac has been taunting us all along! Look at this... he even signed the data entry... BNM."

Mike had walked up the board and looked where Jake was pointing.

"Son of a bitch, Jake, I think you're right."

"I know I'm right. He's not dead. He faked his death and he's been calling the shots on this whole thing."

Mike looked at Jake.

"Jesus Christ, Jake, he must have been the one that hired 'The Agent.'"

"So what's he going to do now?"

Just then, Clark walked in. He was carrying a duffle bag in one hand and a cup of coffee in the other.

"Clark, what are you doin' here?"

"Burke called me. He had me e-mail all the reports and told me to stay here and see this thing through."

Clark looked at the board, and then at Jake and then at Mike.

"What's goin' on?"

"You're not gonna believe this one," said Mike.

"What?"

Jake spoke up. "Our buddy, Benjamin Matthews, he's still alive."

Clark seemed stunned and dropped the cup of coffee he had been drinking onto the floor.

"What? The guy died of a heart attack in prison."

"He faked his death," said Jake. "Son of a bitch is out there alive and he's still playing with us. He's the one who's after Fletcher and the Castro brothers. He must have hired 'The Agent.'"

"Jake, that's impossible."

"I only wish it was. But the plot is just as twisted as Matthew's brain."

143

And Jake showed him the evidence: the initials of the 'Birth of New Madrid', the way the e-mail was signed, and the information they received from Mr. Monroe in New England.

"I'll be a son of a bitch!" said Clark. "This guy's amazing, and I walked right into it."

"Don't feel bad, Clark," said Jake, shaking his head. "This guy was running circles around me for a long time 'til I finally got to him."

At that, Clark smiled.

"Listen, guys, I've gotta e-mail this information to Burke right away."

"Not yet, Clark. This stays with us until I notify the President."

Just then, Jake noticed the duffle bag on the floor, and looked at Clark.

"This is the rest of the stuff from 'The Agent's' apartment. Where do you want me to put it?"

"Just hang it on a peg by the evidence board, Clark."

"Anything else you need me to do?"

"Not yet. We'll have to figure out what this bastard's next move is now that 'The Agent' has been taken care of. I can't see him just walking away from this."

Clark looked thoughtful, looked up at Jake, and said, "No, probably not. I'll be around when you need me."

Clark looked again at the evidence board and then stared at Jake.

"You certainly are one quick study to figure this one out. I'll give you that." And he left.

Jake looked at Mike, who was staring at the evidence board.

"Jake, you honestly think Matthews would hire an assassin to take out the President and the Castros?"

"Why not?"

"Because that leaves out something very, very dear to our former Attorney General."

"What do you mean?"

"Jake, do you really believe that if he had the opportunity, he wouldn't take us all out? You think there's anyone he hates more than you? And Jake, I gotta tell ya, this assassin thing's been bothering me from the beginning, you know that. And I swear, when we opened that door and walked into that room, that guy fired his gun into the ceiling because he meant to, and I swear to God I heard him say 'Happy Birthday'. Jake, it's like it was a setup."

Now Jake was staring at the board.

"Mike, what'd you just say?"

"It seemed like a setup."

"No, before that, when you were talking about Matthews."

"What do you mean?"

"Hired an assassin… Mike, you said former Attorney General… former AG."

And with that, Jake took the marker and circled the first two letters of the word "Agent."

Jake stared and said, "B-N-M-A-G. Benjamin N. Matthews. Attorney General. It's too close to be a coincidence. He set it up. The whole fuckin' thing's been a setup! You were right, Mike. He's been playing us the whole time. But this guy wasn't an assassin; he was a pawn in the game. There is no goddamn 'Birth of New Madrid' organization, there is no goddamn 'Agent'!"

"Which leaves us with a big problem," said Mike.

"Yeah, I know," said Jake. "What's the son of a bitch really gonna do?"

They both stood there and looked at the evidence board.

"Mike, look at the e-mail, that first data entry. Look what it says. 'The Hawk and the Doves will soar but then be consumed in the pit of Hell'. Mike, he's going to blow it up."

"Blow what up?"

"Everything... the whole goddamn park!"

"How Jake? We've got it covered."

"No, we've got it covered from land, sea, and air, but not from underneath—'the pit of Hell'. Eva, come in here!"

"What is it, Jake?"

"I need you to do something real quick. Get City Public Works on the line. I need the diagrams for the drainage system underneath North Shore park, and I need them yesterday. Have whoever you talk to check their files 'cause I want to know the names of the last ten people that signed those plans out."

In five minutes, Eva walked back in the room.

"Jake, it's going to be coming in on fax. A nice elderly lady at the Department of Public Works was kind enough to do so after I informed her that if she didn't pay attention to me, I was going to have the President of the United States call her and chew her ass out."

Mike looked at Jake. "The woman has a way with words."

Eva smiled at Mike and said, "Thanks, sweetie," and went back out to the office.

When the faxed blueprints came in, they assembled them on the conference room table but first looked at the sign-in sheets.

Jake pointed out to Mike, "Look—the last entry. M. N. Benjamin."

"No one can ever say the bastard isn't ballsy," said Mike.

Knowing full well that they were now on to Matthews' plan, they reviewed the blueprints carefully, following the maze of pipes that had formed the underground drainage system from Collins Avenue before the revitalization of North Shore Park.

"All right, Mike," said Jake, "You said you were familiar with this. What are we looking at here?"

"Jake, I was only familiar with the fact that it used to be an underground drainage system. As far as how this thing runs, I don't know. But here is the intake, and this looks like the metal grate that prohibits access to this alcove where all the pipes split off."

"What's this square marking?"

"That's the drain grate where Paula tripped, at the southern end of the park near that abandoned parking lot. That's directly above the metal grate that forms the entranceway to the pipe system."

Jake committed the fact to memory and moved on.

"Let's juxtapose this with our diagram for the treaty signing ceremony."

Mike went to the mapping board they had been using, pulled off the diagram for the podium, dignitary section, seating, etc. , for the ceremony and placed it next to the underground diagram of the park. Using the inlet, that was marked on both, as the starting point, and a ruler to adjust the scale, they followed the underground pipe system. Jake gasped audibly as he realized what Matthews intended to do.

"Mike, look—the pipe—look where it ends."

"Jake, it's right beneath the speaker's podium. If you put enough C-4 under there, it will take out anyone at the speaker's podium and anybody within a fifty yard radius."

Jake looked at Mike.

"And that would include all the dignitaries, and all the guests including you, me, and my family. You were right again, Mike. That's been Matthews' plan all along. He isn't just after the President or the Castro brothers—he's after us. He wants total revenge, and this allows him to get it."

Jake went to the phone. "Eva, get me the commander of the Seal demolition squad that's out on the Coast Guard ship."

Jake turned around and looked at Mike. "We're going to stop this son of a bitch again Mike. We have the upper hand this time.

He doesn't know that we know about this. He has to be running this with a remote detonator or timer. Either way, he's not planning to set this off until the ceremony, sometime around noon, day after tomorrow. We will send in the Seal team tonight and they can diffuse this thing. We have him beat."

"What if he has a backup plan? The son of a bitch does tend to think ahead."

"That's what worries me too," said Jake.

Just then, the phone rang.

"Commander, this is Jake Sullivan. Listen, I need you to get your team assembled and put 'em in the water. You need to go to the inlet at the southern end of the park. I know, I know it's patrolled every hour. Listen to me, here's where you have to go, and this is what you're gonna find."

And with that, Jake laid out the details of what he knew the team would find once it entered the inlet and made its way through the pipes. On the other end of the phone, Commander Edward C. Masik listened as Jake provided him with the information he would need.

Making sure he was clear on the details, he repeated what he understood, and told Jake, "Mr. Sullivan, we're on it. I'll put the team into action immediately and report back to you as soon as we confirm that the threat has been cancelled."

On the other end, Jake thanked him and told him to move as quickly and with as little fanfare as possible, explaining that with the ceremony being day after tomorrow, he wanted to keep this situation under wraps. He also wanted to make sure the commander understood the main objective, but also to check all the other pipelines that ran underneath the park to make sure there was nothing there.

Once both Jake and Masik had ensured their mutual understanding of the mission, Masik signed off and turned to his second in command. "Assemble Squad D on deck. Be prepared for full demolition recovery and wait for my instructions. Clear the deck of anyone other than Squad D."

"You want the deck cleared, Commander?"

"You heard me. Now move it!"

"Aye, aye, sir."

Masik looked at the faxed printout of the inlet and the maze of pipelines running beneath the park before he headed out on deck to meet with Squad D.

That evening Jake and Mike waited in the office, alternately drinking coffee, pacing back and forth, cursing Benjamin Matthews, and damning themselves for not realizing his plan sooner.

"Well, Mike, at least you can be happy that you haven't lost your old instincts for the FBI. You didn't like that assassin story from the beginning."

"Yeah, but I gotta tell you, Jake, I never in a million years would have thought this was Matthews. You figured that one out. It's crazy. Matthews could have pulled it off if he hadn't let his ego get in the way and our good friend Mr. Monroe hadn't called. He had to put his signature on everything. He couldn't make it anonymous, he wanted someone at some point to go back and figure out it was him. Without your discovery we'd have figured we had gotten the bad guy and everything would have been fine until we were all blown to Hell."

Jake looked at Mike.

"Yeah... I am kinda glad we avoided that scenario."

Mike had just finished saying, "We haven't avoided it yet," when Commander Masik's call came through. It was 9:00 p.m. exactly.

"Mr. Sullivan, this is Commander Masik. Mission accomplished. The main objective was found, the mechanism was disarmed, all other pipelines under the park were searched and nothing else was found in any of them. But I have to tell you, there was no need for anything to be in any of the other pipelines. There was enough C-4 wired together where you indicated it would be to blow that whole park to shambles. The timer was set to detonate at noon on the day of the treaty signing ceremony. The whole mechanism, after being diffused, was put in a sealed, water-tight container and taken back to our Coast Guard vessel where it's being analyzed now to see if we can come up with anything as to whom the perpetrator or perpetrators might be."

"Commander, I need you to do me a favor. I need you to hold that order. Keep the materials under seal in your possession and yours alone until I call for them to be delivered to this office."

"Mr. Sullivan, are you sure?"

"Commander, I appreciate everything you've done and I know this may seem like an odd request, but I'm acting with the authority of the President of the United States and for now, this has to be something that remains between you, me, and your team, and no one else. Are we understood?"

There was silence for a while.

"Yes, Mr. Sullivan. Understood. Call when you need the materials delivered to you, and until then, they will remain safely secured in my possession."

"Thank you, Commander, and once again, I appreciate all your assistance, and please complement your team from me on a job well done."

"It will be a pleasure, Mr. Sullivan. Thank you."

"Thank you, Commander," and with that, Jake hung up. "They got it. The site's safe."

Mike let out a sigh of relief. "So what now, boss?"

"Now I have to call Jason Bates and tell him I need the President in my office first thing tomorrow morning when he lands in Miami. I have to assemble the security details and let them know everything that's happened."

"I don't think Bates is going to go for that. Doesn't the President have a full schedule tomorrow with all the dignitaries and the Castro brothers coming in?"

"I'm sure he does. But he's going to have to make time for this, and when I tell him a certain someone has returned to the land of the living, I don't think he's going to give me much argument."

Mike shook his head. "I think you may be right."

CHAPTER 29

Jake called Jason Bates and informed him that it was essential for the President, and all the members of the security teams that had been assembled for the ceremony, to come to his office as soon as Air Force One landed in Miami on the following day.

"Jake, that's impossible. The President is scheduled to meet countless dignitaries tomorrow, and he also has a meeting with the Castro brothers to go over everything that needs to be done before the actual signing of the treaty, with the respective delegations from the United States and Cuba all present."

"Jason, I know the President is going to be especially busy tomorrow, but I'm telling you that you and everybody else need to learn what has happened. Let me make it brief. Benjamin Matthews is alive. The whole assassin plot was a ruse to keep us away from the real threat to the President, which was enough C-4 in the pipe system underneath the park to blow everybody you've just talked about into small, unidentifiable pieces. I think that's something the President needs a briefing on before he meets with the dignitaries and the President of Cuba and his more famous brother, don't you?"

There was silence.

"Jake, you have evidence for all of this?"

"Jason, I have enough C-4 to take out the Coast Guard ship where it's presently stored in the possession of Commander Masik. Masik led the Seal team that went into the pipelines underneath the park to diffuse and retrieve the explosives. I will show you the evidence I have that Benjamin Matthews is alive, and I will show you the evidence we have that the assassin was a ruse to distract us from the bomb threat. And I will show the President because I expect him to be here in my office tomorrow morning as soon as possible."

"All right, Jake, you win," said Bates. "We'll be there. Air Force One is scheduled to land at 7:15 a.m. Have everyone assembled in your office at 8:00, and I'll have the President there. Make sure you keep the meeting short Jake. He will still need to take care of everything else he has to do."

"Short and sweet it will be," said Jake. And with that, the line went dead.

True to his word, Jason Bates and Jordan Fletcher, the President of the United States, walked into Jake's office in Miami at 8:00 a.m. sharp the following morning. Jake had already assembled all the members of the security teams, including Tom Burke and Jonathan Clark from the Secret Service. Earlier, he and Mike had posted the evidence they had gathered in their investigation into the assassination threat against the President and the Castro brothers on a large board. The security personnel questioned why they had been called in the day before the ceremony when they all had things to do, and Jake and Mike told them everything would be explained upon the arrival of the President. The fact that the President was coming made most in attendance realize that something major had occurred or was going to occur and it ended their questioning. They all sat in silence waiting for the President's arrival.

When Jordan Fletcher walked through the door, everyone stood up and Fletcher immediately moved his hands in a downward motion.

"Sit... sit... sit. All right, Mr. Sullivan. You wanted me here, I'm here. I hope you realize my schedule is a little cramped today, so what you have to tell me better be good."

"I know, Mr. President," said Jake.

"All right, Mr. Sullivan, get to it," said the President.

"Thank you, sir."

And Jake went through everything that he and Mike had discovered since the day before. He reminded the group how this entity, the 'Birth of New Madrid', had no prior history, how it had come into being, it seemed, solely for this event. He detailed the information that he received about 'The Agent' and how this heretofore unknown and unheard of assassin became common knowledge to the team assembled in this room, with all the details necessary to ensure that they were able to identify a man they've killed as 'The Agent'.

"You can thank Mike Lang," said Jake. "He never quite believed the assassin theory and his concern is what led us to uncover the real plot."

He then pointed out how Benjamin Matthews' initials were the same as the signatory for the data entry about the 'Birth of New Madrid'.

He went over the phone call he received from Mr. Monroe, the caretaker of the cemetery where Matthews had been buried, and he went over his realization that the beginning letters of *Agent*, A-G, stood for Attorney General, and established that the whole plot had been concocted by Matthews. Matthews had faked his death in prison and sent them all on a wild goose chase for an assassin that didn't exist, had set up the alleged assassin in an apartment with conveniently placed information that identified him as 'The Agent', while his real plan was to blow up the President, the Castro brothers, and everyone assembled in the room, at the time of the treaty signing ceremony. He explained that they were in the process of trying to identify the body of the man who had been believed to be 'The Agent'.

He provided diagrams of the piping system and the park and explained how Commander Masik and his team had located and removed the C-4 that had been directly beneath the podium in sufficient amounts to annihilate anything within a fifty-yard radius, with a detonation time of noon tomorrow. The C-4 was currently being stored on a Coast Guard ship under the direct surveillance of Commander Masik.

At that moment, Jonathan Clark leapt out of his chair and screamed, "You son of a bitch!"

All heads yanked around to Clark, including that of the President, stunned by the outburst. Clark looked like he was somewhere else, staring in the direction of Jake Sullivan, a look of rage on his face, his fists clenching and unclenching at his sides. Tom Burke reacted.

"Clark, what are you doing?!"

His words seemed to bring Clark back to reality. Clark seemed to make a visible attempt to calm himself, closing his eyes and breathing in deeply.

"Mr. President... Tom... everyone here... Jake... I apologize. My outburst was directed to Benjamin Matthews. I'm the one that brought you the information, and if Mr. Sullivan here had not had the ability to once again thwart another scheme of this madman, everyone in this room could have been dead by noon tomorrow. I let myself be played. I was so sure that I had discovered something so important that I never looked at the other possibilities. I never felt the sense that something wasn't right, that Mike Lang had. I let my emotions get in the way of my reason..."

something I never do. I apologize to everyone assembled here for my actions in this matter, and I want to congratulate Mr. Sullivan on once again saving the day. Tom, my resignation will be on your desk this afternoon."

"Clark wait!" started Burke.

"Tom, my decision is final."

And with that, Clark stormed out of the room, knocking chairs aside as he went, his fists clenching and unclenching in unfettered rage.

When Clark was finished, there was stunned silence in the room, broken by President Fletcher, who stood up.

"Everyone keep their seats. Mr. Sullivan, once again you have provided me with a detailed briefing, and based upon our past relationship, I believe it to be true. I want every law enforcement agency in this country to quietly and without fanfare institute a worldwide manhunt for Benjamin Matthews. Mr. Sullivan, I agree with what you have done in keeping this matter under wraps. I want this monster given no publicity, and I want the world to continue thinking he is dead until we have once again placed him under arrest, when we will quietly put him back into prison for the rest of his life. Thanks to Mr. Sullivan and Mr. Lang once again, a major threat to our country has been eliminated. They, and all you in this room, have my thanks for all your efforts."

Speaking to Director Tom Burke of the Secret Service, the President said, "Tom, I want you to go and find Clark, make him understand that this isn't his fault. Matthews has duped a great many people over his career, myself included, and make sure you tell him I said that. He's proved himself in the past to be a fine agent, and I want him to continue in the service. Tell him that his resignation is not accepted by the President of the United States. Gentlemen, thank you again. I have work to do. Tomorrow is a historic day."

At that point, Jake Sullivan spoke up. "Mr. President, before you leave, please, a word of caution, and this is to everyone in this room, Matthews is still out there. We think we've discovered the real threat he had in place and neutralized it. But as the President said, Matthews has led us down many paths in the past and there could be something else out there, so everyone needs to stay alert. All security plans are still in effect, all details will receive their assignments as planned, and all security will continue at a heightened status. Anything out of the ordinary, and I mean anything, no matter how trivial it may seem, needs to be reported by your men to you and then to Mike and me. We have to make sure there's nothing else up this madman's sleeve. Sorry to keep you, Mr. President."

"It was worth listening to, Jake. Thank you once again."

Bates looked at Jake, nodded, and smiled, and then the President, Bates, and their security detail were out the door.

The head of Homeland Security stood up and began to applaud. The rest of those seated in the conference room joined in, and Jake raised his hands in embarrassment.

"All right, all right . . . enough, enough. Nothing to clap about. This isn't over yet. Let's go make sure that tomorrow's historic for all the right reasons. We have a great President to protect."

And with that, Jake and Mike left the room.

CHAPTER 30

It was midafternoon. Jake was sitting in his office. The board from the conference room had been brought back in and he was staring at it. He was going over everything again and again in his mind—this whole scenario as it played out. He knew he should be ecstatic. As Mike had said after they had left the meeting, "Well boss, I think you have their respect now."

Jake replied, "I think *we* have their respect, Mike. You earned it as much as anyone," and they had shaken hands.

Mike was in one of the other offices getting briefing reports as they were submitted to him on an hour-by-hour basis, which would continue up until the time of the treaty signing. They came in by coded e-mail and Mike would review them. No response from Mike or Jake was required unless something was amiss and both Jake and Mike hoped that they would not be required to respond. They both new they were in for a long night and a long day tomorrow.

They had stopped the bad guy once again, but Jake still was bothered by something. He had always had the ability to remember facts—dates, names, conversations—not a photographic memory, but a pretty good one. And he trusted his gut; it usually signaled when something wasn't quite right, when something was out of place. He was missing something. He knew it dealt with the evidence he had been staring at all this time.

He stood up and walked to the board. He went from document to document to document, moving from right to left, from the first data entry that established the credentials of the 'Birth of New Madrid' to the other end of the board where Clark had tied the sack with the evidence from the alleged assassin's apartment on the hook. He knew it was there, but he couldn't see it. Shaking his head, he decided it was time to get away for a minute, go splash some cold water on his face, get something to drink, go for a walk … anything … and then come back and start all over again. He took one last look before he walked out the door.

"Damn it!" he thought. "What is it?"

It was eating at him because deep down inside he knew it was important. Shaking his head again, he walked out the door, headed out of the suite of offices of the Justice Department and headed to the men's room down the corridor.

The corridor was quiet today. The only people in sight were a U.S. Marshall, who was face to face with someone he had brought in under arrest. The suspect was sitting in a chair with his hands handcuffed behind his back. The Marshall barely acknowledged Jake as he passed, speaking in a whisper to the man seated in front of him.

Jake walked in to the men's room, relieved himself, splashed cold water on his face several times, and looked into the mirror. The face that stared back at him showed the exhaustion of the past several months. The dark brown hair had a smattering of gray around the edges. There was a strong jaw with a cleft in the center. The blue-green eyes showed sympathy and caring, but also showed an edge and a sense of purpose. Wiping his hands and face dry with a paper towel, he exited the men's room and went down to the alcove where the vending machines were located and bought a cold Diet Coke.

He was drinking the Coke on his way back when he looked at the Marshall and the handcuffed man sitting in the chair, and that's when it hit him.

To the Marshall's surprise, the Chief Prosecuting Attorney of Miami went by him in a sprint. He passed through the outer offices and ran into his office, slammed the Coke can down on the desk, and moved toward the board, staring at it, but it wasn't there. That had been his problem. He wasn't looking in the right place. He hadn't been listening, either.

He went to the duffle bag that Clark had tied on the peg and stared at it for several minutes, then ran over to his desk and fumbled through all the stacks of paper until he found what he was looking for—a photograph. He took the photograph, went over, and once again looked at the duffle bag hanging on the hook.

He went over to the phone and dialed. There was only one ring before the line on the other end came alive, and he heard the voice of Tom Burke.

"Burke... Secret Service."

"Tom, this is Jake Sullivan. Did you have a chance to talk to Clark?"

"Not yet Jake. I couldn't catch up with him. He was gone. I've been trying to get a hold of him, but he's not answering his cell phone. I think this thing has really devastated him."

"Tom, let me ask you a question. When we first talked about this, you had told me that you had been upset with Clark because you said he went dark while he was out gathering information. What did you mean?"

"We have a system whereby agents, if they are out in the field doing investigative work, have to file reports and call in on a regular basis. We didn't hear from Clark for over a month. There was an occasional e-mail, but that was it."

"Do you know where he was all that time?"

"Primarily in Mexico. He said that's where he found the source for the data entry point that led him to this whole 'Birth of New Madrid' thing. Obviously, that's where Matthews was, that's where he entered the data."

"Do you know exactly whereabouts in Mexico he was?"

"I think it was somewhere near Acapulco… somewhere down in Baja, California."

"All right Tom, thanks."

"What's this about Jake?"

"Nothing yet. Just trying to put some final pieces together on this thing. I'll be back to you. Thanks."

And with that, he hung up. The phone had barely hit the cradle when Jake was again running out of the office, heading down the corridor and punching the down button on the elevator. Jake paced in front of the elevator, silently cursing his failure to realize what had been going on all along. He waited for the elevator doors to open. After what seemed like an eternity, they did, and Jake sprang in and pressed the button repeatedly for the basement. It seemed to take forever for the elevator to crawl down the sixteen floors to the basement level where the evidence locker was located. Jake was out the door as soon as it opened, heading for the locker. He knew the guard on duty.

"Hello, Mr. Sullivan. What can I do for you?"

"Sully, I need to look at the evidence on the Benjamin Matthews case. Tell me where it's located."

"That's the last thing I think you need, Mr. Sullivan. Given that the bastard finally did us all a favor and died."

"Sully, it's important. Where is it?"

"Okay, Mr. Sullivan, okay. It's aisle three, boxes one through ten."

"Buzz me in Sully."

With that, the locked cage door opened, and Jake moved back through the maze of metal racks full of cardboard boxes containing evidence from various Justice Department prosecutions. He found aisle three and moved down, scanning as he went, and finally came upon the boxes that stored the evidence on Benjamin Matthews. They were all marked and Jake finally found the one that said *Materials From Office*.

Pulling it off the shelf, he dropped it on the ground, ripped open the tape, and rummaged through until he found a photograph in a frame. He stared at it.

Looking back at boxes stacked before him, he saw the box labeled *Materials from Lab* at the very top. He found the rolling ladder, dragged it over, climbed up and grabbed the box and brought it down to the floor.

Tearing it open, he rummaged through until he found what he needed and ran back out.

"Thanks Sully. Left a little mess back there. I'll take care of it later."

"But Mr. Sullivan..."

But before Sully could say anything else, Jake was gone, heading back to the elevators, which eventually took him back to his office.

He reached into one of the trash cans, sifted through, and pulled out a paper cup. He sat it on his desk. Ripping the back off the picture frame, he yanked the photograph out of the frame, picked up the other photograph he had been looking at, and walked over and looked at the duffle bag one more time. He walked back and collapsed in the chair behind his desk, afraid to trust his chain of thoughts.

He ran through everything again—every word that had been said, everything that had been done, the information he had received and where it had come from. As wild as it was, he was sure.

Jake slowly walked out to the outer office, one hand on his hip and the other running through his hair, trying to come to grips with the magnitude of what he had discovered, and trying to decide what he was going to do.

Turning around, he realized that Eva was sitting there, staring at him—obviously nonplussed by his running back and forth.

"Jake, are you all right?"

"I don't know, Eva. I don't know."

"What do you need me to do?"

"Come on in my office for a minute, Eva."

Jake walked in, rubbing his eyes, and looked at Eva.

"I'm sorry about all the running around out there, Eva. I know it must look like I'm a crazy person."

"Jake, stop. I've seen you in action before—somethin's going on and it's important. How can I help?"

"Eva, I need you to do something for me, but you can't ask me why, and you can't tell anyone else about it. It has to stay between you and me, all right?"

"Whatever you need, Jake."

With that, he handed her a document he had removed from the lab results box in the Matthews' files, and the coffee cup from the trash can.

"This coffee cup has DNA on it. I need it compared to the DNA sample in these lab results and I need it immediately... and by immediately, I mean now. I want you to personally take this downstairs to the lab and tell them exactly what I just said. I want everything else stopped. If you get any argument from anyone, get me on the phone."

Eva looked at the name on the lab report she was holding in her right hand and then looked to the paper coffee cup in her left. A look of dread came over her face as she raised her head to Jake.

"Oh, Jake—he's not..."

"Eva, remember, no questions. Just do this for me, all right?"

Eva swallowed hard and nodded. Jake came to her and put his arms around her shoulder and hugged her.

"I'll take care of this, Eva. Don't worry, I'll take care of this. Just get me that information, all right?"

Eva looked up at him and said, "I will Jake. I won't need to call you. I'll get you your information, and I'll get it now. Promise me one thing."

"What's that?"

"That you'll be careful."

"I will, Eva. I promise. Now, do me one more favor before you start. Find Mike and tell him to come in here, will you please?"

Eva nodded her assent and walked out of the office. As she was leaving, she turned and looked back at Jake.

"Remember, Jake Sullivan, you promised me."

Jake smiled. " I know, Eva. I know."

A few moments later Mike walked into the office.

"What's up, Jake? What's Eva so upset about? She told me to get in here as fast as I could. She looked like she was ready to cry."

"Sit down, Mike. I've got a story to tell you."

"Oh no, a story from Jake Sullivan I have to sit down for. I know I'm not going to like this."

And with that, Mike took a chair.

"All right Mike, you're not going to believe this. Just bear with me as I go through this, all right?"

"I'm all ears."

"Mike, you remember this picture?" Jake said showing him the picture he had removed from the frame from the office evidence box.

"Can't say that I do Jake."

"This is the picture that was confiscated from Matthews' office when he was the Attorney General. I retrieved it from the evidence room downstairs."

"And?" said Mike.

"And, look what's in the picture."

"It's a kid sitting on a dock. There's a boat behind him."

"Look more closely. Look how the boat's tied to the dock."

"It's with a rope."

"Look at the knot, Mike. Look at the knot."

"Jake, I don't get it. What are you trying to tell me here?"

"Look, when I was a kid growing up in Pennsylvania, a retired Navy man used to live in the house next to us, and on summer days when I didn't have anything else to do, I would sit on his porch and he'd take a couple pieces of rope and he'd show me how to make all the Naval knots he had learned throughout his career. I'd practice and I'd practice so I could get them right, and he taught me the names of all of them. That's a Carrick bend. That's a picture of a young Benjamin Matthews with his boat tied up with that particular kind of knot, all right?"

"All right," said Mike quizzically.

"Now, look at this. This is a picture that Jim Nelson gave me about an old case we had worked on."

"O. k. It's a picture of a dead guy," said Mike.

"That dead guy is a plastic surgeon the Mexican police discovered in an underground surgical theater that they had raided thinking it was a drug distribution center. Jim and I had a case with a guy who skipped bail and we lost his trail in Mexico. The word was that he had found a plastic surgeon who had developed a new technique with new types of equipment that could do a complete facial make-over. In less than a month, the wounds heal—everything, ready to go. I think Dr. Simone Lorenza found near Acapulco, Mexico, was that guy."

"Jake, I'm sorry. I'm still not following this."

"Look at the way his hands are tied behind him. Look at the knot."

"Okay. It looks like the same knot on the boat, right?"

"Exactly. Now come here."

He took Mike by the arm and led him to the evidence board.

"Look at the duffle bag that Clark hung on the hook. Look at the knot. It's a Carrick bend."

"The same knot, right?" said Mike.

"Exactly. The knot in the picture, the knot with the dead plastic surgeon, and Clark's knot on this bag are the same type of knot. It's a knot you don't normally see and it's usually used out of habit."

It started to dawn on Mike what Jake was thinking.

"Jake, where are you going with this?"

"Just hear me out Mike. Listen, I was out in the hallway, went to get a Coke, and was walking back. There was a U.S. Marshall talking to someone he brought in, sitting in a chair with his hands cuffed behind him. The Marshall was in his face telling him something, and that's when I remembered."

"Remembered what, Jake? What did you remember?"

"I remembered being in the same position, sitting in a chair with my hands handcuffed behind me with Benjamin Matthews leaning over me... and you know one of the things he told me, Mike? He told me I was a quick study. No one else in my life has ever told me that using those words. The only other time was in this room... yesterday... when Clark told me the exact same thing."

Just then, the intercom buzzed.

"What is it, Eva? Give it to me... okay, thanks. Listen, remember what I said—this is between us. All right, thanks Eva."

"Jake, you can't be thinking..."

"Mike, think about it. Every detail we got about the 'Birth of New Madrid', about 'The Agent'... came from one person... Clark. I talked to Tom Burke. Clark was dark for a month, rarely checked in, clearly against agency policy. He told Burke that during all that time he was somewhere near Acapulco, Mexico, in Baja, California—the same place that this plastic surgeon was killed."

"Jake, are you saying what I think you're saying?"

"It's exactly what I'm saying. Every bit of information we got in this investigation that pointed us to the 'Birth of New Madrid' and 'The Agent' came from Clark. Clark's the guy that shot the presumed assassin down before we could talk to him. You remember Dave Thomas when he was here? Said that Clark was ambidextrous, but that he was really left handed? He was surprised that Clark was wearing his gun on his right side. If someone accessed the *real* Clark's records to get details about him, it would say he was ambidextrous, not that he was really left-handed, and they'd think continuing to use their right hand would be okay. It flashed on me, that when we went out to try and arrest 'The Agent,' I threw Clark the keys to my car. He reached the whole way across his body to catch them with his right hand, same as you did when I threw you the keys to my car—because you're both right-handed! If he was really ambidextrous, it would have been much easier to grab them with his left. And Clark's the guy refers to me with the one phrase I've only heard from one other person in my life... Benjamin Matthews, right before he was going to kill me. When I first met Clark, there was something about him and I couldn't figure out what it was, and now I know. It's the one thing you can't change through plastic surgery Mike—it's his eyes. Mike, it's him. Jonathan Clark is Benjamin Matthews."

Mike went back to his seat and plopped down, shaking his head, looking at the ground.

"Jake, slow down a minute. You got a lot of circumstantial evidence here that you're putting together in a string to come up with something that is totally unbelievable."

"Not any more, Mike. I have science on my side."

"What do you mean?"

"That call from Eva . . . when I was down in the evidence locker getting that picture, I got Matthews lab results . . . his DNA test. I had Eva take it down-stairs and they ran a comparison on a cup Clark had used that I fished out of the trash can. Remember when he spilled it yesterday? I checked it for DNA. It's a 95% positive match to the DNA of Benjamin Matthews. Mike, they're the same guy. Matthews has been here all along. Think about it. Think about how this crazy son of a bitch's mind works, Mike. What could be better for him . . . being here with us, running this scam on us and seeing it happen, watching us run around like chickens with our heads cut off, puppets while he's pulling the strings . . . what could be better? When he stood up in that meeting this morning, he was talking about me. When he found out that I'd unraveled another one of his schemes, he just couldn't take it anymore and he exploded. That whole resignation story crap . . . that was just a cover to hide the real reason why he flew into a rage, and the real reason was that once again we ruined his plans."

Now Mike was up pacing.

"Jake, you gotta be kidding me. You're tellin' me the whole time that no good rotten son of a bitch was here . . . I'm working with the guy? I can't believe this!"

"It's true, Mike."

"How did he pull this off?"

"Think about it, Mike. This guy gained control of the whole drug distribution system in this country. He was the Attorney

General—one of the most powerful men in government. Who knows who he has working for him? He could have people inside the prison, people supplying him with the C-4... he had a lot of contact with a lot of bad people. Who's to say he couldn't have ways to hack into the computer systems and enter whatever data he wanted us to find? If he has access to secret bank accounts and cash stashed away for his use, people will do what he asks for the right price. And we know he has no compunction about killing people after they are no longer useful."

"Who else knows about this, Jake?"

"Right now, just Eva. And that's the way it's going to stay. When I talked to Burke, he couldn't get hold of Clark—he wasn't answering his cell phone and he couldn't find him anywhere. I don't know whether he's gone underground, whether he's left Miami... hell, whether he's left the country... or, if he's hanging around and he's still going to take his shot."

Mike said, "So, what we have to do is find a way to make him show himself."

"You're right, but how?"

CHAPTER 31

Mike and Jake thought long and hard about how to bring Matthews out in the open, and Jake finally convinced Mike of his scheme.

"Jake, I'm tellin' you I don't like this. It's too dangerous. We have to come up with another way."

"Mike, we've been over this. I have to let Matthews know that I know he and Clark are one and the same. If I do that, the game's still going on for Matthews. Right now, as far as he knows, it's over. And if he is planning anything else, with that ego of his and the way he likes to play these games, he'll drop some hint of it. And if he's still after the President and the Castro brothers, maybe we can figure how and we can stop him. If he stays underground and he has something planned, there's no way on Earth we can prevent it between now and tomorrow morning. And with any luck, I can goad him into coming after me . . . and if he comes after me, we can set a trap for him and we'll get him."

"Yeah, we'll set a trap with you as bait."

"Mike, it's the only way. You know that a big part of this was getting me, as well as the President. I have to make him think I'm still available to him."

"All right. I don't like it, but I think you are right," said Mike. "Make the call, see what happens."

Jake punched in the speed dial for Clark's cell phone and as expected, it went straight to voicemail, so Jake left him a message.

"Hey Clark, I just wanted to let you know... you're not as smart as you think you are. I know who you are, Clark. You and I aren't done yet. I'm still here. Come and get me, you arrogant bastard!"

And with that, Jake pressed the End button and sat down behind his desk.

"Now what?" said Mike.

"Now we wait and hope that he calls."

It only took fifteen minutes. Mike and Jake both startled when the phone rang. Jake had given instructions to Eva not to answer the phone—that he would take all his calls himself. He pressed speaker and answered.

"Benjamin, so nice of you to call."

There was silence, then a brief chuckle.

"Hello, Jake. By the sound of things, I must be on speaker phone, so I guess I should say hello to Mr. Lang, too."

"Fuck you, Matthews!" said Mike.

"Always direct and to the point, Mr. Lang," said Matthews. "So tell me, Jake... how'd you know it was me?"

"You know, you're not going to believe this Matthews, but it was a picture of you when you were a little kid with your boat."

There was silence and Jake knew Matthews was thinking, going over the picture in his mind, and then Matthews had it.

"It was the knot, wasn't it?"

"Old habits die hard, Matthews."

"Was it just the one on the duffle bag?"

"No, you got a little unlucky there. One of my associates found out about the murdered plastic surgeon in Acapulco. You used the same knot on him, didn't you?"

"Ahhh... the good Doctor Lorenza. After his services were no longer needed, I determined he was too much of a liability. So rather than pay him his exorbitant fee, I decided to terminate the contract. And once you had the information about the plastic surgeon, it led you to..."

Jake interrupted, "Clark. He was in Mexico at the same time... who gave us all our leads... who sent us on all the wild goose chases... who sat here and enjoyed it so much and who told me, as only you did before, that I was a quick study."

"However, you must admit, you can't claim complete victory on this one. Had that country bumpkin from Rhode Island, Mr. Monroe, not called you, who knows if you would have figured it out on your own."

"Yeah, Monroe gave us a break, but it was your own ego that did you in."

"Jake, you have to realize that there's an amusing side to this. Of course, I did my homework. I knew there was a certain amount of Spanish influence in the elite class of Cuba who didn't like the brothers Castro. But, obviously, I made up the name of 'Birth of New Madrid' simply because it conformed to my own initials. I was simply amazed when Ms. Cortez gave her presentation and gave credibility to something I had simply made up. Sometimes I think I'm actually smarter that I really am."

"And had your plan worked, you had to give people a way to figure out that you were behind everything. You knew damn well that someone would figure it out after they studied that information long enough."

"Yeah, but of course, the important thing, Jake, is you and that idiot Fletcher and everybody else would have been dead by then... so it really wouldn't have mattered, would it? Oh well, it's better that we all know who we all are now, isn't it?"

"You set up everything, didn't you, Matthews?"

"Of course I did, Jake. It really wasn't that difficult. You would be amazed at the medications that you can take that mimic a heart attack . . . that slow down the heart enough to keep you alive but so a routine examination won't even show a pulse. Just sprinkle a little on your food, ingest it, and there you are."

"I know you were the person entering the false data into the security services computer system, and I presume that's how you found out that you and Clark were somewhat of a match."

"Just a little technology I had installed when I was Attorney General, Jake. You never know when you might need these things. Access to important information is a way of life these days, and I wanted to make sure I stayed on top of things."

"Wait a minute!" said Mike. "When Clark . . . or I guess you . . . gave that presentation about the data entry, you said you were the one giving the techs directions for the creation of the firewall and all that other bullshit, but you would already have been in Mexico."

"Mr. Lang, you really must keep up with the latest in computer technologies. When I was Attorney General, I found an amazing technician who taught me everything he knew about the subject. Unfortunately, after he did, he died in a terrible motor vehicle accident. So, there really wasn't anyone who knew I had such knowledge. You see, Mr. Lang, if you know what you're doing, you can sit at a computer terminal in Acapulco, Mexico, and the people you're dealing with on the other end of that computer can believe that you're sitting at a threat analyst's desk in the Secret Service Agency. You just have to know how to press the right buttons, shall we say. I'm trying to make it as simple for you as possible."

"The Hell with you, Matthews! You're not nearly as clever as you think you are."

"You'll have to admit, Mr. Lang, that certainly hasn't been the case so far in our little adventure."

"And Clark, I presume . . ." said Jake.

"Jake, you know the answer to that question. We couldn't have two of us running around, now could we? So, once Dr. Lorenza did his work, and my associates were able to get all necessary data from Mr. Clark to make sure I could take his place, it really would have been messy to leave him around. Let's just say he's found a permanent home in the warm waters off Mexico."

"And, of course, you were the person who went into the art store that the girl reported on. You were the guy who somehow brought the man we believed to be 'The Agent' to that apartment. Did you wear a disguise when you went to get the building plans, too?"

"Of course, Jake. It was all me. I must admit, I passed myself off quite well as an artist and a construction worker, by the way. And that poor guy I shot was just a homeless out of work laborer. Believe me, he won't be missed—no family… no one to care about him."

"So what are your plans now, Matthews?"

"Well Jake, unfortunately, you've ruined things again. I was having so much fun watching you scurry about, following all those leads to all those clues. I thought you were going to blow a gasket with that little delay we had about the information on our infamous assassin, but I made sure the information would come in late, just to put you a little more on edge. Remember Jake, I know you. As we got closer to the date of the great ceremony and you couldn't find our assassin friend, it was starting to wear on you. I'm surprised you didn't go get yourself a couple Coronas. But no, you're the strong hero type, aren't you, Jake? No more insecurity… no more vices. You put away the bad guy, and now you're on top of the world. So, Jake, the grand finale I had planned for the President and those scumbags from Cuba will no longer take place. What a gala it would have been… fireworks and everything. Historical proportions, I would think. But now I'm left performing only a minor spectacle. You see, I just have to take care of some family business. Then, I think I'll disappear again for a while, and then maybe I'll come back Jake. Think about that. You'll never know when... you'll never know where... but I promise you, I'll be back. And Jake, trust me, there are a lot of people out there like Lorenza, so you'll never see me coming. Just go to bed each night with the thought that I am coming Jake... and if it makes you feel any better, I want you to know... I don't really give a damn about the President and those idiots from Cuba... my real target has always been you. You're the one who ruined my life... and yours is the one I intend to ruin. Till later, Jake!"

And with that, the line went dead. Mike got up and slammed both hands on the desk.

"What an arrogant prick! I can't wait until we get a hold of this guy..." Mike stopped and looked at Jake.

"What is it, Jake?"

"The news release when they said he was dead... it said he had no living relatives, Mike. What family business is he going to take care of?"

Reading each other's minds, Jake and Mike immediately headed for the door, Jake speed dialing Linda and the girls, all of whom were staying at Linda's house in preparation for the ceremony tomorrow.

"Christ Mike! He means my family!"

"Keep calling while we're moving," said Mike. "Let's get to the house."

Jake tried Linda's cell phone... no answer. As he was running out of the office, he looked at Eva.

"Eva, keep calling Linda and my daughters. If you get hold of them, tell them to get here to the office right away, and when they get here, put a guard on them."

"Jake..."

"It's what I thought, Eva. Get some security up here now, and you stay here, too."

As Jake was heading out the door, he heard Eva call behind him.

"Jake! Remember... you promised me!"

As they entered the hallway, Jake heard the elevator bell ding, and he headed for it.

Mike ignored the elevator and headed for the steps leading to the garage.

Jake reached the elevator door just as it was closing. He hollered, "Keep that goddamn door open!" He reached out, trying to get his fingers in the narrowly closing space, but it was too late. The door closed and the elevator began its descent. Cursing his luck, he turned, ran to the steps and started down.

Upon reaching the basement, Mike had jumped in his car, gunned the ignition, and pulled out into traffic. Ignoring the cars around him, the tail of his car was struck by an approaching vehicle. Ignoring the collision, the angry shouts and honking horns, he headed for Linda's house in Coconut Grove, praying to God he would get there in time.

Jake burst into the garage and jumped into his car. As he went to pull out of the garage, the entrance was blocked by the traffic snarl that Mike had created. Cursing and pounding his hand on the horn, he hollered for the owners of the various vehicles now stopped to get out of his way. When no one would comply, he hit the accelerator and pulled out directly into the traffic snarl in front of him, smashed into the front end of the car that had hit Mike, as well as another car, causing another round of angry shouts from the owners. Ignoring the chaos, he extricated his car from the mess and sped down the street. Mike was nowhere to be seen. Jake's elevator gambit and the traffic snarl put him ten minutes behind.

It was twenty minutes before Jake pulled up in front of Linda's house and saw Mike's car parked half on the drive and half in the yard, the motor still running. Jake double-parked in the street, jumped out of the car, and headed for the front door. His heart dropped as he saw the door was open and slowly walked in. He had taken the Glock 17 from his glove compartment. The Justice Department had issued it to him after the Matthews affair and Jake had spent time on the range getting comfortable with it. He was an accurate marksman. The first thing he did when he got in the car on his way over here was take it out, take out the clip, check to make sure the sixteen rounds were there, one in the chamber, and then he slammed the clip back into place.

Jake slowly pushed the door open and entered the darkened house. The blinds had all been pulled and sunlight was rimming the edges, giving some visibility but not much. He was about to turn right when a sound came from his left.

"Jake... in here."

The voice was low and in pain, but Jake knew it was Mike, and he went to his left, his gun still out in front of him held in both hands at eye level.

As Jake turned the corner, he saw Mike on the floor. He scanned the room to make sure no one else was there and went and knelt down beside Mike.

"Jake, I'm sorry. I got here too late. He was waiting for me. As soon as I opened the door, he got me. I think he shattered my shoulder. Jake, I'm sorry... he has the girls."

"Linda?"

"Yeah... Linda too, Jake. I'm sorry."

Jake's mind raced. The thought of his wife and children in the hands of Benjamin Matthews sickened him, and he began to tremble uncontrollably with both fear and rage, until Mike grabbed his arm with his good left hand.

"Listen… listen to me Jake… get me up and we'll go after them. Nothin's going to happen to your wife and children. We'll get 'em. There's a cell phone on the table. He said when you got here to hit redial. Jake, I think it's the only reason he left me alive. Jake, he's really insane now. After he shot me, he stood over me and put that gun to my head. Then he said, 'One player's down… should I make it permanent, or not? No. Let's let him live. He can give Jakie-boy a message.'"

"It's all right, Mike. It's all right. Just lay there and be still. I'll get you some medical help. You're not going anywhere."

Jake reached for the phone, but Mike grabbed his arm again.

"Jake, listen, you have to know… he has explosives. He made necklaces. He has one on Linda and on both the girls."

Jake's eyes closed. His fear and fury were about to overwhelm him, but he steadied himself and a steely resolve took over. He was going to end this once and for all. Matthews had hurt his friend. He had let him live, but only out of a perverse sense of humor. Jake had no sense of humor. Matthews had his family. He planned to see him dead.

Jake punched redial and waited. The voice came on the line.

"Hello, Jake. I guess you found your friend."

"So this is the way you're going to do things now, Matthews? You ambush people, then prey on women and children?"

"Please, Jake. No sermons. I told you… you destroyed my life. I'm going to destroy yours. I don't think your investigator is going to be much use to you now with what I did to his shoulder. And I imagine he's already told you about your wife and kids…"

"Matthews, I swear to God! If you hurt them in any way!"

"Jake, Jake, Jake, really…you're not in a position to be making threats. Least you forget, I have the detonator. I'm sure Mr. Lang told you your wife and children are wearing brand new necklaces of my creation."

"So what is it Matthews? What do you want?"

"It's obvious Jake—I want you. You are going to meet me and we're going to have a family reunion."

"Why, so you can kill us all?"

"Jake, I give you my word. I promise you, that I intend to leave you and your family alive and well as I ride off into the sunset. What more could you ask of me?"

Jake stalled for time, thoughts rushing through his head.

"All right Matthews. I'll meet you, but I'm picking the place. I don't trust you."

"Like I said Jake, I really don't think you're in a position to dictate terms... but for the sake of argument, I'll listen. Where would you like our little rendezvous to be?"

"At the southern end of North Shore Park near the old abandoned parking lot. You bring my wife and children, and I'll come alone, unarmed."

"Jake, it's not that I don't trust you... but I don't trust you. Although, I must admit, there is a lovely irony to meeting you at the site where I intended to blow you all up. All right, Jake. I'll agree to your request, but on my conditions. I'll have the detonator for the explosives that are hanging around the necks of your wife and two daughters taped to my hand. So, let's say if a sniper decided to put a bullet in my head, I'd still have enough reaction time to hit the plunger before I went down. If someone tried to grab me, the detonator wouldn't fall out of my hand. So, make sure you are alone, Jake. No security personnel. No guns, no hidden weapons of any kind. If I am convinced, I will reunite you with your family, as I promised."

Jake looked at his watch. It was almost six o'clock. He did some quick calculations in his head.

"All right Matthews. My security details are expecting me to walk the perimeter and go over last minute details at 9:00 o'clock tonight. I can tell them that I have a meeting with Jonathan Clark that has to be strictly private and for them to hold their positions and to allow no one to interfere with that meeting. I can also get you clearance through the guards that patrol the entrance to the abandoned parking lot at the southern end of the park. So let's say we meet at 10:00."

"Ten o'clock it is, Jake. By the way, just so you know, I took the liberty of gaining access to all your phones, Mr. Lang's phone, all the other equipment in your office. If you call anybody about this situation, I'll know. And if I hear such a call being made, I'm afraid the reunion I promised you simply won't happen. So, we have a couple hours to wait Jake. It will give me time to get to know your lovely wife and daughters."

"Matthews, I'm tellin' you . . . if you hurt them in any way . . . "

"Jake, again with the threats. What do you think you're going to do? And besides, Jake . . . I gave you my word."

"I want to talk to them Matthews . . . I want to know they're all right."

"A fair request, Jake, a fair request."

Jake's emotions raced from excitement in hearing Linda's voice back to despair knowing the situation she was in and how scared she must be.

"Jake, it's all right. I'm all right."

"Linda . . . Linda . . . It'll be okay. We'll get through this."

"Jake, don't do what he wants. Stay away."

"Give me that phone!" Jake heard Matthews say.

"Here girls, talk to daddy."

"Girls, are you all right?"

They answered in unison, although he could hear the fear in their voices and imagine the tears in their eyes.

"We're fine daddy. We're okay. Don't listen to this jerk. Stay away daddy. Stay away."

The next thing he heard was Matthews' voice.

"Feisty little group you have here, Jake, I must admit. This is going to be more fun than I thought. See you at ten," and with that, the line went dead.

Jake couldn't help but think, his heart bursting with pride, "That's my wife and kids—worried more about me than about themselves."

If Jake wasn't sure before, he was sure now—he was going to save them.

Jake looked down at Mike.

"Hang in there, Mike."

He used the same phone to dial 911 and requested an ambulance be sent immediately to Linda's address. Mike looked up at Jake, grimacing in pain.

"I'll be all right, c'mon. Jake, get me up. I'll help you with this."

"No, no. Not this time, buddy. You're gonna sit this one out. I need you to get that shoulder fixed. Regardless of what Matthews thinks, I need you, which means you gotta get that thing taken care of and get back in the line of duty."

"There you go again, Jake. Always worried about me punchin' the time clock."

Jake looked down at Mike and laughed, as did Mike, as best he could given the pain he was in.

Jake waited until the ambulance arrived to make sure Mike was properly treated and taken care of. He told the head ambulance attendant, "Listen, I want him to get the best possible treatment there is, but I want a complete blackout on this. Take him in under a John Doe." Giving him his business card, Jake said, "Don't let anyone know who he is. If anybody has any questions about that, give them this card and tell them to call that number. Do you understand?"

The ambulance attendant looked at the card and then back at Jake and said, "No problem, Mr. Sullivan."

"Thanks. I appreciate it. Now get him to the hospital."

Mike called out from the back of the ambulance, "Jake!"

Jake ducked down and crawled in beside Mike.

"All right Mike . . . they're takin' you to the hospital. I gotta go do some things."

"Jake, listen to me. I don't know what you're plannin' on doin' but you gotta do two things for me."

"What's that, Mike?"

"End this . . . once and for all . . . and walk into my hospital room with your wife and kids healthy and happy."

Jake patted Mike's arm.

"You got it. I'll be seein' you soon."

And with that, he exited the ambulance, shut the back doors, and signaled for the driver to take off. Sirens wailing, it took off down the street, headed for Mercy Hospital.

Jake got back in his car, threw the car into gear, and headed down the street. He didn't stop until he found the nearest convenience store. He pulled in and bought a throwaway cell phone. He got back in his car, opened the binder that was on the seat, found the number he needed, and punched it in.

The voice on the other end said, "Commander Masik."

"Commander, this is Jake Sullivan."

"What can I do for you, Mr. Sullivan?"

"I need some information . . . I need your help."

"Another mission, Mr. Sullivan?"

"Yeah, but this time the mission's mine."

CHAPTER 32

All was quiet at the park when Jake arrived at about 8:30 that evening. After making his cursory inspection, he informed the guards stationed along the perimeter fence created by the orange construction webbing that he was holding a private meeting that evening with Jonathan Clark of the Secret Service down by the inlet to discuss a potential issue that had come up in that area. He told the guards to maintain their positions and ensure that his meeting was kept private.

Jake knew from his previous surveys of the park that there was a significant drop off as the park went south toward the inlet. His reasoning for ensuring that Mike post a guard at the grate where Paula had tripped was because he could not see the perimeter fencing from that area when he looked back to his north and he had wanted to make sure that area was secured on the day of the ceremony.

He had also instructed the guards at the entrance of the old abandoned parking lot to expect Clark's arrival and to allow him access to the lot.

Once he was done with all these details and ensured that the guards were satisfied by his explanations, he moved into his position. But not before he assured himself that Commander Masik's team had done as he had asked. Everything was confirmed when he looked down at the area behind him and when he felt a slight tug on his pant leg.

As he stood there, Jake looked long and hard to the north. He had been correct. The terrain obscured the orange webbing of the perimeter and he knew that the guards would not be able to see his interaction with Matthews.

He went over again and again in his mind the information the Commander had provided him, and he prayed that his plan would work. The lives of his wife and children depended on it.

Jake had listened closely to the words Matthews used when they had last spoken. Matthews had promised them a family reunion and he had promised to leave them all alive and well, but Jake had no illusions. He knew exactly what Matthews was planning. Through whatever means, Matthews was going to incapacitate him and reunite him with his wife and girls. Matthews would then leave and when he was a safe distance away, he would detonate the bombs that were around the necks of his family. Simple and sick. Matthews had been chagrined that all he was left with was a "small spectacle" but doubtless he took great comfort in the fact that Jake and his family were to provide that spectacle; what better way to ruin Jake's life than have him sitting there helpless, knowing that he and his family were going to die.

The key was the detonator. Jake could take no chances in trying to get it away from Matthews. Matthews had been right about his reaction time even if a sniper did take him out. And in a scuffle between the two of them, it could be pressed by accident.

There was only one thing Jake could think of to do, and the Commander confirmed he was right.

So, now all Jake could do was wait for ten o'clock and for Matthews and his family to arrive.

Jake held his position and finally heard the car engine. He looked at his watch, which showed it was a quarter to ten. He was staring out at the ocean. He turned around to see a panel van pulling into the lot, and he watched as Jonathan Clark exited the driver's side door of the van and started walking toward him.

Jake was wearing a slim fitting dark jersey and dark pair of pants, with no place to conceal a weapon. He put his hands up over his head.

"Hello, Jake. Beautiful evening, isn't it?" said Matthews as he approached.

"Where's my family, Matthews?"

"They're safe, Jake, inside the van. I'm going to take you to them, as I promised I would."

"I kept my word, too, Matthews." "No guns, no weapons, no phone calls—no one here except you and me."

"As it should be, don't you think, Jake? We both knew this was how it had to end—between you and me. It's been that way ever since I first started coming down to Miami when I was Attorney General. It's always been between you and me."

"Let's end it that way then, Matthews—just you and me. Leave my family out of this."

"Jake, you know I can't do that."

Jake took a few steps forward, as if to lunge at Matthews.

"Ahh, ahh, Jake. Back up! Back up! Remember what I told you."

And Matthews held up his right hand. There it was, the detonator flashing its red light, duct taped to his hand.

"See Jake, if this light goes green, everybody goes boom! And that's not what we want, is it?"

In truth, Jake did back up, counting his steps as he did so. He turned as if in exasperation, looking at the ocean, but actually, he was making sure of his position.

"Matthews, what's with you and these games? Let's just get this over with, can we? I want to see my family!"

"All right, Jake, here's how it's going to work. You're going to hold out your hands, I'm going to slip these plastic handcuffs over them and you're going to walk in front of me to that van."

With that, Matthews pulled out a pair of double-cuffed disposable handcuffs, something commonly used by Federal Marshalls. Nothing new to Jake.

"And as I promised, I'm going to reunite you with your family and I'm going to walk away. And when I do, true to my word, you will all be alive and well."

"All right, Matthews—let's play it out to the end."

With that, Jake held his hands out in front of him. Matthews approached.

"Turn around, Jake. I want to take a good look at you and make sure you're keeping your end of the bargain."

"I told you Matthews, no weapons, no phones, no wires, nothing . . . just as you had asked."

Jake turned around in a complete circle, coming back to face Matthews.

"Jake, you are a man of your word. Now hold out your hands."

Matthews approached, holding his right hand with the detonator away from his body and somewhat behind him, out of Jake's reach. With his left hand, he slipped one of the plastic handcuffs over Jake's right hand and pulled it tight. As he went to put the other handcuff on Jake's left hand, Jake shifted his stance. Moving his hand slightly, the handcuff slipped off his left hand before Matthews had the chance to tighten it, and Matthews tried to grab it before it slipped out of reach. Jake knew it was his moment—the only one he would have—and he fell straight backwards, pulling Matthews with him, headfirst, holding onto the handcuff that had been firmly attached to Jake's right hand.

"Please God..." thought Jake, "Only a couple seconds... that's all I need."

As Matthews fell, fingers splayed, he reached out with his right hand to regain balance, for a second he was distracted from the detonator in his hand, and by the time he realized what Jake had done, it was too late and they were in the water.

The Commander's team had done an excellent job in sabotaging the drain grate that Paula had tripped on. A laser cut on the rusted lock that held the grate in place gave way as the weight of the bodies hit.

Jake had worked it out with the Commander. They had calculated that Jake's call for a ten o'clock meeting was perfect –the tide would be at its highest and its roughest.

They hit the water and were immediately submerged. The tug that Jake had previously felt as he was waiting for Matthews to arrive, was a Navy Seal reaching up from beneath the grate to grab a safety line that Jake had attached to a belt he was wearing and concealed in his pant leg. The Seal had then attached the safety line with a clasp to one of the rungs of the ladder before leaving the cavern.

It was pitch dark and all sounds were obscured by the tide, pulling at them both so that they were horizontal in the water, their feet pointing toward the inlet, the tide sucking at them, trying to draw them out. Matthews was now hanging onto Jake's handcuff for dear life while frantically pushing the detonator button on his right hand—but the Commander had been right about that, too. He had assured Jake that the type of detonation device that Matthews would have would be for surface use. The electronic impulse would need to travel through the airwaves, and that water would destroy the device's ability to find the airwaves and, ultimately, deactivate the device. It was the only option Jake could come up with to safely disarm the device with the least risk to his wife and children. It had worked.

Even in the darkness, Jake had been able to see the red light, praying that it would not change to green, and it had not, and eventually, the red light had gone out.

But Matthews wasn't going to give up. He knew again that he had been duped... that once again, Jake had gotten the best of him, and he was in a furious rage. His rage powered against the pull of the tide. Pulling himself up along the handcuff strap until he had Jake by the arm, he struck out at him with his fists and legs. Jake was able to fend off the weak blows. But Matthews kept coming, until finally, he had his hands around Jake's neck. He hoped to drown him, even if it meant killing himself.

Held by the tether line, Jake brought both of his hands up between Matthews' outstretched arms and pushed forward, forcing Matthews' hands from around his neck. Matthews gripped Jake's shirt with his left hand and struck at him with his right. Jake fought back, hitting Matthews as best he could with the purchase he had. Finally, he felt Matthews weaken and at that moment, Jake gave one fierce kick, breaking the surface of the water and gasping for as much air as he could. He reached up to the concrete encasement with his left hand and grabbed hold. He slid his left hand along the surface of the concrete, keeping his grip secure while at the same time reaching out with his right hand, trying to find the U-bolt that secured the grate. Secured to the U-bolt, just as planned, was a holster containing a Glock 17.

Suddenly, Matthews broke the surface of the water and threw his arm around Jake's neck, trying to pull him backwards. Jake only saved himself by grabbing the concrete encasement with his right hand and holding on with both hands. Jake knew it was a battle he could not win. Matthews was cutting off his air and, weakened from the fight, Jake knew he could not resist Matthews' leverage for long. He turned slightly, took his right hand from the concrete encasement, and, with every ounce of strength left in his body, he elbowed Matthews directly in the face. Matthews' grip relaxed. In that instant, Jake reached out again with his right hand and there it was... the butt of the Glock. He managed to wrap his hands around it and grab it just as Matthews, no longer stunned, yanked at Jake with everything he had and brought him back under the surface of the water. Fighting fiercely as they went under, Jake twisted to face Matthew and forced the Glock between them. He pulled the trigger twice. Bubbles erupted and Jake felt Matthews grip loosen. Even in the dark, he could see the shadow spreading in the water and he could feel a slight temperature change. Finally, he pushed Matthews away, and in an instant, the tide did its work. Benjamin Matthews was gone.

CHAPTER 33

Exhausted and aching from Matthews' blows, Jake pulled himself along his safety rope to the steel ladder, made his way up the rungs, and broke the surface of the water, filling his lungs with air. He then continued up the ladder until he reached the grate's concrete encasement.

Even though Jake has seen the light on the detonator go from red to nothing, he prayed every rung he went up. While under water, and even when he broke the surface, the tide was so loud that he couldn't tell whether he had been successful... whether somehow the detonator had gone off.

As Jake climbed, his senses were keen. The acrid smell after an explosion was not in the air. There were no sounds of emergency vehicles... no sounds or smell of crackling and burning metal. As Jake brought himself up, he straddled the concrete edge of the grate and rolled over onto the grass. Raising his head, he looked in the direction of the van and slowly struggled to his knees.

As promised, the Commander's team had been waiting for Jakes' move, and when Jake dragged Matthews down through the drain grate, they immediately went to the van, opened it, and consoled Jake's wife and daughters, watching for the instant that the lights on the necklaces went out. Removing the necklaces, tears and hugs were exchanged by three terrified women and a group of strong, battle-hardened men.

Jake got up from his knees and slowly rose. His legs were like rubber, but with each step he took, they became stronger. He broke into a run. As fast as his legs could carry him he reached his wife and children and gathered them all in a large embrace. They cried and he cried. They hugged and they kissed, and Jake told them how sorry he was for what had happened. They told him that they were all right and how happy they were that he was safe and alive. His daughters looked at him and told him that they knew he would come, and they knew he would save them. Jake looked at Linda and saw in her eyes love and fear, pride and worry, but most of all, there was relief... relief that they were all alive, all still here together.

CHAPTER 34

October 28th was a beautiful, warm Miami morning. Jake tried to listen intently to the words of President Fletcher. He tried to comprehend the historical significance of the event, and was somewhat in awe seeing Fidel Castro no more than twenty feet before him on American soil.

It was hard for Jake to concentrate. His mind kept going back through the events of the past several months and, particularly, the events of last night. He looked over at his wife and daughters, who, in typical fashion, had insisted that they attend the ceremony regardless of what they had gone through.

After their emotional outpouring, Commander Masik insisted they go to the hospital to be checked, and Jake had readily agreed, the only caveat being that they go to Mercy Hospital, where he knew Mike had been taken, so that he could check on his good friend.

Masik had insisted in having his team accompany them to ensure their safety, and again, Jake did not object.

When they arrived at the hospital, they found that Mike had already gone through surgery, was awake and in post-op.

Commander Masik came up to Jake before they went in to the emergency room to be checked and held out his hand.

"Mr. Sullivan, it's been a pleasure. Any time you want to take a crack at joining my Seal team, I'll be happy to give you the opportunity."

Jake smiled and took the Commander's hand and shook it firmly.

"Commander, trust me… I know my limitations, but I sincerely want to thank you and your men for everything you've done, not just for your country… not for the President… but for me and my family."

Before he turned to walk away, Commander Masik looked at Jake.

"As I said before, Mr. Sullivan, it's been a pleasure. Take care of those young ladies for me."

"I intend to, Commander, I intend to."

Jake, Linda, and the girls were checked out at the emergency room. Other than the emotional trauma, Linda and the girls had some slight bruising around their necks and wrists but there was no indication of any other type of injury.

Jake appeared to have at least one cracked rib and bruises all over his body, but other than that, he, too, was none the worse for wear.

With dry clothes magically acquired by Commander Masik, Jake and his family made their way to the recovery area. They walked in to find Mike sitting up in his hospital bed, his shoulder heavily bandaged, with Eva on one side of the bed and Paula on the other.

Jake whispered to Linda and the girls and they immediately went to Mike's bedside, taking up position where Eva had been, who ran to Jake and threw her arms around him, repeating over and over again, "Thank you, Jake… thank you… thank you."

Jake looked down into her face.

"What are you thanking me for, Eva?"

"For keeping your promise, Jake ... for coming back safe. Jake, is it ..."

"Yes, Eva. It's over."

Eva again hugged him tightly, and then took his hand and moved him towards Mike's bed.

"The girls were just filling me in on your little escapade. They must have been exaggerating. You don't look that bad."

"I sure as hell look better than you," said Jake.

"That's because I took one for the team."

Jake became serious looking at Mike.

"Yes, you did ... and I wish you hadn't had to."

Mike, in a rare moment, became serious, too.

"I wish I could've been there with you for this, Jake. I'm sorry you had to do it alone."

There was a knowing look between Jake and Mike as Eva said, "All right boys, enough of this! Things are much better when you two are fighting and cussing at each other."

And with that, everyone in the room laughed.

Eva said to Mike, "It's time to let you get some rest. I'll check in on you tomorrow."

"Thanks, Eva. I appreciate it."

Jake spoke up. "I have to get these girls home to the warmth and safety of their own beds. I know you're in good hands here with Paula. I'll check in on you later."

And with that, Jake turned to escort his family out of the room.

"Jake!" Mike called out.

Jake turned, a questioning look on his face.

"I thank you for keeping your promise, too."

Jake just looked at Mike and nodded and smiled.

Not too much later, back at Linda's house, Jake quietly closed the door to the room the girls were sleeping in and slowly walked down the hallway to Linda's bedroom, his body aching as he did.

He crawled into bed beside his wife and she immediately rolled into his embrace, and they lay there like that... silent for a long time.

"Linda, I'm so sorry about what happened. I should have figured out Matthews' plan earlier. I should have figured out who Clark really was. I should have prevented all this."

Linda sat up on the bed facing Jake, holding his hand.

"Jake, you saved us. You ended this. You did what you had to do." She shook her head and said, "Jake, I know you're always there, and will always be there to protect us... it's just that..."

"What is it?"

"It's just that things are different. I know you never planned on your relationship with the President, but Jake, he does trust you. He is going to call on you for things. Sometimes those things are going to put you in danger. Jake, I knew when I married you what kind of person you were. I know you don't walk away from a fight. I know you can't let bad things go on without trying to change them. I know the type of person you despise. You've always said you can't stand cheats, liars, cowards, and bullies, and usually when you find one of those characteristics, you find them all. I know you can't walk away from that type of person.

But, Jake, this is different. You're drawn into situations now that put you in real danger, and tonight my worst fears were realized... it put the girls in real danger. Jake, you saw how they are. You saw how they acted. You've instilled in them that courage and that sense of right and wrong that you have. They were more worried about you than they were about themselves. The problem is, Jake, I can't do that. I can't worry more about you than I do about them. They're our children. Jake, what if someday I have to choose? How do I do that? How do I protect you and them at the same time? How do we all live, never knowing what's coming? Jake, I'd never ask you to change... I'd never ask you to stop doing what you love . . . but I just don't know if I can put the girls through it anymore. I don't know if I can take that risk . . . that risk of them being hurt. Jake, I love you, and I'll always love you, but I just don't know . . ."

And Jake lay there, holding his wife as close to him as he possibly could, knowing that her words were true, and dreading what they meant.

EPILOGUE

The treaty ceremony went off without a hitch, a historic event extolled around the world.

There was no mention at the ceremony or any time thereafter of the events of the days and night before the treaty signing ceremony. The President, Jason Bates, and all involved agreed that it was best that Benjamin Matthews remain buried.

A few days after the treaty signing, one Carl Monroe of Providence, Rhode Island, opened his door to find the Coast Guard standing there, informing him that they had the cremated remains of Benjamin Matthews in their possession, positive identification having been made, and would Mr. Monroe please be so kind as to re-inter Mr. Matthews' remains in the proper plot at St. Anne's Cemetery at the expense of the federal government. Mr. Monroe was all too willing to oblige, and the ashes of someone known as Benjamin Matthews now rest forever at St. Anne's.

Jonathan Clark was posthumously reinstated to the Secret Service, and his name now adorns their wall of honor with those agents who died in protection of the President and in service of their country. Unfortunately, he was gunned down in Little Havana trying to locate the whereabouts of a purported assassin. The perpetrators of his death were never captured.

Every morning, Clyde Johnson would tell anyone who would listen who came to purchase coffee or a newspaper what a good man Mr. Clark had been and what a tragedy it was that his life was taken. Most of those who knew of his death would agree.

It was a beautiful morning in Miami as Jake made his way to the entrance of Mercy Hospital on South Miami Avenue. He stopped outside the door and punched in a number on his cell phone. Eva answered on the other end.

"What can I do for you, Jake?"

"Eva, I'm gonna be a little late this morning. I'm stoppin' off to see Mike."

"Oh, Jake, please give him my best. Tell him I miss him."

"I will, Eva. I'm sure he'll be happy to hear that. What's going on?"

"Jake, you'll be very, very happy to know that everything here is very, very quiet."

Jake chuckled to himself.

"Eva, that's the best news you could've given me. I'll see you when I get there."

"All right, Jake."

And with that, he hung up and strode through the door. He made his way into Room 403 and pushed open the half-closed doors and found a common sight, Paula Cortez sitting on the side of Mike's bed, holding his hand, smiling and talking.

"Hello, kids," said Jake, clearing his throat.

"Hey, Jake," said Mike. "Good to see you."

Paula got up from the bed and came over and put her arms around Jake's neck and hugged him and kissed him on the cheek.

"Jake, I never got to tell you that night when you came to the hospital after everything happened, I'm so glad you're all right. We were so worried about you."

Mike chirped up from the bed, "Speak for yourself, Paula. I wasn't worried. I knew he'd pull it off."

Jake laughed.

"You certainly had more confidence than I had."

"Jake, your wife and kids were on the line. I knew there was only gonna be one outcome."

Jake nodded.

"So, how are we today?"

"Doc says I'm healin' pretty well, actually. Gonna have to go through a lot of therapy, but I should be back in action pretty quickly. I'm thinkin' maybe, you know, couple months vacation, nice beach somewhere, warm sunshine ... probably do a world of good."

"Mike, I already talked to your doctor. You have six weeks of hospital therapy and then you're back to work."

Mike looked at Paula and said, "Well, there go all our plans. Told you we couldn't trust that doctor."

Paula laughed.

"Don't worry Mike. We'll get to the beach eventually."

Jake stood there rocking back and forth with his hands in his pockets, not knowing quite what to say, but Paula understood.

"I think you boys probably need to talk by yourselves. I'm gonna go get a cup of coffee. I'll be back. Can I get you anything?"

"Yeah. How about goin' out and gettin' me a nice warm pizza so I don't have to eat this hospital crap anymore?"

Jake looked at Paula.

"Is he always like this?"

"Jake, he's the worst patient you could imagine."

"Somehow that doesn't surprise me," said Jake.

Paula then left them alone.

Jake walked over to the window quietly watching the blue Atlantic out in the distance sparkling in the sunlight. Mike let him stand like that for a while.

"All right, Jake, I know you too well. What's bothering you?"

"Mike, remember when you came to the boathouse when I showed you Ortiz's body and I told you what I'd done?"

"Yeah, Jake, I remember."

"You never said anything to me about that." He turned and looked at Mike. "Why?"

"Jake, the man lying on the floor, by anyone's definition, was a bad man. You, on the other hand, by anyone's definition, are a good man. That man had caused many people a great deal of pain and suffering. As far as I was concerned, the shot he had taken from Matthews' guard is what killed him anyway. You were just expressing an opinion . . . one you had every right to express."

"I don't know Mike. I did it again with Matthews, and it doesn't seem to bother me. Commander Masik had offered to have two Seal team members under the water, waiting for Matthews when I pulled him under. It would have been a smart thing to do for Linda and the girls, but I refused. I didn't want him subdued . . . I didn't want him captured . . . I wanted him dead . . . and I wanted to be the one to kill him. I'm a federal prosecutor, Mike. I'm supposed to bring people to justice, but I was damned if that son of a bitch was ever going to see the inside of a courtroom. I'm worried, Mike. Ortiz didn't bother me . . . and Matthews doesn't bother me."

"Jake, let me say it again. You're my friend and a good man. You did what anyone would have done."

Jake turned to Mike.

"Would you have done it?"

Mike thought.

"Jake, when I was with the Bureau . . . when I was wearin' the badge . . . I had a duty that I had to follow. I had a right and wrong that was set out for me, not by some moral authority, but by law, and I took an oath that I would do it. I was never faced with your situation. Back then, I probably wouldn't have done what you did. Now... Jake, I honestly don't know. I'm sorry if that's not the answer you're lookin' for, but it's the truth."

"That's all right, Mike. I know who I am. I've learned what I'm capable of. I know that I'll do what I have to do. The sad thing is, Linda knows it, too, and I don't think it's something she can deal with."

"I'm sorry to hear that, Jake. Give her time."

Jake took a deep sigh.

"I don't think that's the issue, Mike. It's not time, it's not lack of love... she's afraid Mike. She's afraid of who I am. She's afraid for her... she's afraid for the girl s... she's afraid for me... and I think living with that constant fear is bad enough, the way we are now. Being together as a family, having that fear there all the time... I don't think she can deal with it." There was a long pause. "At any rate, you get better. When those six weeks are up, I want you back in fighting condition, you understand?"

"Again with the orders. I've been shot! Leave me alone!"

They both laughed.

"All right, I am gonna leave you alone. I've gotta get back to the office."

"Jake, that's not all there is. I know you too well. What else is bothering you?"

"Mike, they never found his body. They searched up and down the coast. They never found him."

"Jake, he could be miles out to sea by now. He could be in the Gulf Stream... headed God knows where. Jake, you shot him. He was in the water. He was ripped through the channel into the ocean... he's dead."

Jake's eyes hardened.

"We've done this before, Mike. Can you say you're sure?"

Mike looked away.

"The thirteenth tropical storm's brewing out there, you know?"

"Shouldn't it be the end of this? It's almost November."

"I hope this is the last one of the season. There's no telling what this one's going to bring."

"Why? What's so different about this one?" said Mike.

"It's the thirteenth storm, Mike... letter 'M'... tropical storm Matthew."